THE ASPERN PAPERS

1800s Venice is the setting for this tale of greed and obsession: a crumbling, beautiful, mysterious place where the incredible becomes real and the strange is almost commonplace. In fervent pursuit of the letters written by a famous deceased poet to a former lover, the anonymous narrator becomes a lodger under a false name in the dilapidated palazzo of the woman and her spinster niece, in the hope of procuring his prize. The resulting clash of wills and cat-and-mouse games among the trio reveal the deepest motivations that drive human nature — and just how far is the narrator willing to go to get what he wants?

Books by Henry James
Published by The House of Ulverscroft:

THE TURN OF THE SCREW

SPECIAL MESSAGE TO READERS

Cox

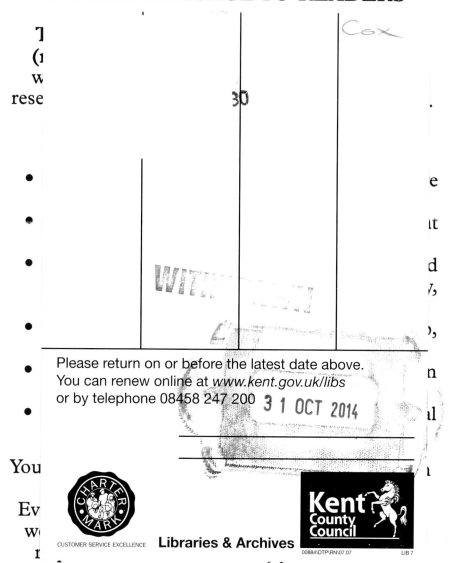

THE ULVERSCROFT FOUNDATION
The Green, Bradgate Road, Anstey
Leicester LE7 7FU, England
Tel: (0116) 236 4325

website: C161006996)ft.com

Born in New York City, Henry James (1843-1916) enjoyed a privileged upbringing, his father being one of the wealthiest intellectuals of the time. Henry's family was connected with prominent American writers and philosophers of the age, including Henry David Thoreau and Nathaniel Hawthorne, all of whom had a profound influence on young Henry. He embarked upon his writing career in 1864, his short stories and novels initially being serialised in American magazines, though he continued his prodigious output after moving to London in 1876. He remained a bachelor all his life and became a British citizen in 1915, the year before his death. Although he was buried in Massachusetts, a memorial stone was dedicated to him in Westminster Abbey. He is remembered particularly for his well developed characters; his social commentary on politics, class and status; and his exploration of the themes of personal freedom, feminism and morality. His stories, which have appeared frequently on stage and film, have never been out of print.

HENRY JAMES

THE ASPERN PAPERS

Complete and Unabridged

ULVERSCROFT
Leicester

First published in Great Britain in 1888

This Large Print Edition
published 2014

A catalogue record for this book is available
from the British Library.

ISBN 978–1–4448–2002–7

Published by
F. A. Thorpe (Publishing)
Anstey, Leicestershire

Set by Words & Graphics Ltd.
Anstey, Leicestershire
Printed and bound in Great Britain by
T. J. International Ltd., Padstow, Cornwall

This book is printed on acid-free paper

1

I had taken Mrs Prest into my confidence; without her in truth I should have made but little advance, for the fruitful idea in the whole business dropped from her friendly lips. It was she who found the short cut and loosed the Gordian knot. It is not supposed easy for women to rise to the large free view of anything, anything to be done; but they sometimes throw off a bold conception — such as a man wouldn't have risen to — with singular serenity. 'Simply make them take you in on the footing of a lodger' — I don't think that unaided I should have risen to that. I was beating about the bush, trying to be ingenious, wondering by what combination of arts I might become an acquaintance, when she offered this happy suggestion that the way to become an acquaintance was first to become an intimate. Her actual knowledge of the Misses Bordereau was scarcely larger than mine, and indeed, I had brought with me from England some definite facts that were new to her. Their name had been mixed up ages before with one of the greatest names of the century, and they now lived obscurely in Venice, lived

on very small means, unvisited, unapproach-
able, in a sequestered and dilapidated old
palace: this was the substance of my friend's
impression of them. She herself had been
established in Venice some fifteen years and
had done a great deal of good there; but the
circle of her benevolence had never embraced
the two shy, mysterious and, as was somehow
supposed, scarcely respectable Americans — they
were believed to have lost in their long exile
all national quality, besides being as their name
implied of some remoter French affiliation
— who asked no favours and desired no attention. In the early years of her residence
she had made an attempt to see them, but this
had been successful only as regards the little
one, as Mrs Prest called the niece; though in
fact I afterwards found her the bigger of the
two in inches. She had heard Miss Bordereau
was ill and had a suspicion she was in want,
and had gone to the house to offer aid, so that
if there were suffering, American suffering in
particular, she shouldn't have it on her conscience. The 'little one' had received her in
the great cold tarnished Venetian *sala*, the
central hall of the house, paved with marble
and roofed with dim cross-beams, and hadn't
even asked her to sit down. This was not
encouraging for me, who wished to sit so fast,
and I remarked as much to Mrs Prest. She

replied, however, with profundity: 'Ah, but there's all the difference: I went to confer a favour and you'll go to ask one. If they're proud you'll be on the right side.' And she offered to show me their house to begin with — to row me thither in her gondola. I let her know I had already been to look at it half a dozen times; but I accepted her invitation, for it charmed me to hover about the place. I had made my way to it the day after my arrival in Venice — it had been described to me in advance by the friend in England to whom I owed definite information as to their possession of the papers — laying siege to it with my eyes while I considered my plan of campaign. Jeffrey Aspern had never been in it that I knew of, but some note of his voice seemed to abide there by a roundabout implication and in a 'dying fall.'

Mrs Prest knew nothing about the papers, but was interested in my curiosity, as always in the joys and sorrows of her friends. As we went, however, in her gondola, gliding there under the sociable hood with the bright Venetian picture framed on either side by the movable window, I saw how my eagerness amused her and that she found my interest in my possible spoil a fine case of monomania. 'One would think you expected from it the answer to the riddle of the universe,' she said;

and I denied the impeachment only by replying that if I had to choose between that precious solution and a bundle of Jeffrey Aspern's letters I knew, indeed, which would appear to me the greater boon. She pretended to make light of his genius and I took no pains to defend him. One doesn't defend one's god: one's god is in himself a defence. Besides, today, after his long comparative obscuration, he hangs high in the heaven of our literature for all the world to see; he's a part of the light by which we walk. The most I said was that he was no doubt not a woman's poet; to which she rejoined aptly enough that he had been at least Miss Bordereau's. The strange thing had been for me to discover in England that she was still alive: it was as if I had been told Mrs Siddons was, or Queen Caroline, or the famous Lady Hamilton, for it seemed to me that, she belonged to a generation as extinct. 'Why, she must be tremendously old — at least a hundred,' I had said; but on coming to consider dates I saw it not strictly involved that she should have far exceeded the common span. None the less she was of venerable age and her relations with Jeffrey Aspern had occurred in her early woman-hood. 'That's her excuse,' said Mrs Prest half sententiously and yet also somewhat as if she were ashamed of making a speech so little in the real tone of Venice. As if a woman needed an excuse for having loved the divine poet! He had been not only one of the most brilliant minds of his day — and in those years when the century was young, there were, as every one knows, many — but one of the most genial men and one of the handsomest.

The niece, according to Mrs Prest, was of minor antiquity, and the conjecture was risked that she was only a grand-niece. This was possible; I had nothing but my share in the very limited knowledge of my English fellow-worshipper John Cumnor, who had never seen the couple. The world, as I say, had recognised Jeffrey Aspern, but Cumnor and I had recognised him most. The multitude today flocked to his temple, but of that temple he and I regarded ourselves as the appointed ministers. We held, justly, as I think, that we had done more for his memory than any one else, and had done it simply by opening lights into his life. He had nothing to fear from us because he had nothing to fear from the truth, which alone at such a distance of time we could be interested in establishing. His early death had been the only dark spot, as it were, on his fame, unless the papers in Miss Bordereau's hands should perversely bring out others. There had been an impression about 1825 that he had 'treated her badly,' just as there had been an impression that he had 'served,' as the London populace says, several other ladies in the same masterful way. Each of these cases Cumnor and I had been able to investigate, and we had never failed to acquit him conscientiously of any grossness. I judged him perhaps more indulgently than my friend; certainly, at any rate, it appeared to me that no man could have walked straighter in the given circumstances. These had been almost always difficult and dangerous. Half the women of his time, to speak liberally, had flung themselves at his head, and while the fury raged — the more that it was very catching — accidents, some of them grave, had not failed to occur. He was not a woman's poet, as I had said to Mrs Prest, in the modern phase of his reputation; but the situation had been different when the man's own voice was mingled with his song. That voice, by every testimony, was one of the most charming ever heard. 'Orpheus and the Maenads!' had been of course my fore-seen judgement when first I turned over his correspondence. Almost all the Maenads were unreasonable and many of them unbearable. It struck me that he had been kinder and more considerate than in his place — if I could imagine myself in any such box — I should have found the trick of.

It was certainly strange beyond all strangeness, and I shall not take up space with attempting to explain it, that whereas among all these other relations and in these other directions of research we had to deal with phantoms and dust, the mere echoes, the one living source of information that had lingered on into our time had been unheeded by us. Every one of Aspern's contemporaries had, according to our belief, passed away; we had not been able to look into a single pair of eyes into which his had looked or to feel a transmitted contact in any aged hand that his hand had touched. Most dead of all did poor Miss Bordereau appear, and yet she alone had survived. We exhausted in the course of months our wonder that we had not found her out sooner, and the substance of our explanation was that she had kept so quiet. The poor lady on the whole had had reason for doing so. But it was a revelation to us that self-effacement on such a scale had been possible in the latter half of the nineteenth century — the age of newspapers and telegrams and photographs and interviewers. She had taken no great trouble for it either — hadn't hidden herself away in an undiscovered hole, had boldly settled down in a city of exhibition. The one apparent secret of her safety had been that Venice contained so many much greater curiosities. And then accident had somehow favoured her, as was shown for example in the fact that Mrs Prest had never happened to name her to me, though I had spent three weeks in Venice — under her nose as it were — five years before. My friend, indeed, had not named her much to any one; she appeared almost to have forgotten the fact of her continuance. Of course Mrs Prest hadn't the nerves of an editor. It was meanwhile no explanation of the old woman's having eluded us to say that she lived abroad, for our researches had again and again taken us — not only by correspondence but by personal inquiry — to France, to Germany, to Italy, in which countries, not counting his important stay in England, so many of the too few years of Aspern's career had been spent. We were glad to think at least that in all our promulgations — some people now consider I believe that we have overdone them — we had only touched in passing and in the most discreet manner on Miss Bordereau's connection. Oddly enough, even if we had had the material — and we had often wondered what could have become of it — this would have been the most difficult episode to handle.

The gondola stopped, the old palace was there; it was a house of the class which in Venice carries even in extreme dilapidation the dignified name. 'How charming! It's grey and pink!' my companions exclaimed; and that is the most comprehensive description of it. It was not particularly old, only two or three centuries; and it had an air not so much of decay as of quiet discouragement, as if it had rather missed its career. But its wide front, with a stone balcony from end to end of the *piano nobile* or most important floor, was architectural enough, with the aid of various pilasters and arches; and the stucco with which in the intervals it had long ago been endued was rosy in the April afternoon. It overlooked a clean, melancholy, rather lonely canal, which had a narrow *riva* or convenient footway on either side. 'I don't know why — there are no brick gables,' said Mrs Prest, 'but this corner has seemed to me before more Dutch than Italian, more like Amsterdam than like Venice. It's eccentrically neat, for reasons of its own; and though you may pass on foot scarcely any one ever thinks of doing so. It's as negative — considering *where* it is — as a Protestant Sunday. Perhaps the people are afraid of the Misses Bordereau. I dare say they have the reputation of witches.'

I forget what answer I made to this — I was given up to two other reflections. The first of these was that if the old lady lived in such a big and imposing house she couldn't be in any sort of misery and, therefore, wouldn't be tempted by a chance to let a couple of rooms. I expressed this fear to Mrs Prest, who gave me a very straight answer. 'If she didn't live in a big house how could it be a question of her having rooms to spare? If she were not amply lodged you'd lack ground to approach her. Besides, a big house here, and especially in this *quartier perdu*, proves nothing at all: it's perfectly consistent with a state of penury. Dilapidated old *palazzi*, if you'll go out of the way for them, are to be had for five shillings a year. And as for the people who live in them — no, until you've explored Venice socially as much as I have, you can form no idea of their domestic desolation. They live on nothing, for they've nothing to live on.' The other idea that had come into my head was connected with a high blank wall which appeared to confine an expanse of ground on one side of the house. Blank I call it, but it was figured over with the patches that please a painter, repaired breaches, crumblings of plaster, extrusions of brick that had turned pink with time; while a few thin trees, with the poles of certain rickety trellises, were visible over the top. The place was a garden and apparently attached to the house. I suddenly felt that so attached it gave me my pretext.

I sat looking out on all this with Mrs Prest (it was covered with the golden glow of Venice) from the shade of our *felze*, and she asked me if I would go in then, while she waited for me, or come back another time. At first I couldn't decide — it was doubtless very weak of me. I wanted still to think I might get a footing, and was afraid to meet failure, for it would leave me, as I remarked to my companion, without another arrow for my bow. 'Why not another?' she inquired as I sat there hesitating and thinking it over; and she wished to know why even now and before taking the trouble of becoming an inmate — which might be wretchedly uncomfortable after all, even if it succeeded — I hadn't the resource of simply offering them a sum of money down. In that way I might get what I wanted without bad nights.

'Dearest lady,' I exclaimed, 'excuse the impatience of my tone when I suggest that you must have forgotten the very fact — surely I communicated it to you — which threw me on your ingenuity. The old woman won't have her relics and tokens so much as spoken of; they're personal, delicate, intimate, and she hasn't the feelings of the day, God bless her! If I should sound that note first I should certainly spoil the game. I can arrive at my spoils only by putting her off her guard, and I can put her off her guard only by ingratiating diplomatic arts. Hypocrisy, duplicity are my only chance. I'm sorry for it, but there's no baseness I wouldn't commit for Jeffrey Aspern's sake. First I must take tea with her, then tackle the main job.' And I told over what had happened to John Cumnor on his respectfully writing to her. No notice whatever had been taken of his first letter, and the second had been answered very sharply, in six lines, by the niece. 'Miss Bordereau requested her to say that she couldn't imagine what he meant by troubling them. They had none of Mr Aspern's 'literary remains'' and if they *had* had wouldn't have dreamed of showing them to any one on any account whatever. She couldn't imagine what he was talking about and begged he would let her alone.' I certainly didn't want to be met that way.

'Well,' said Mrs Prest after a moment and all provokingly, 'perhaps they really haven't anything. If they deny it flat how are you sure?'

'John Cumnor's sure, and it would take me long to tell you how his conviction, or his very strong presumption — strong enough to stand against the old lady's not unnatural fib

— has built itself up. Besides, he makes much of the internal evidence of the niece's letter.'

'The internal evidence?'

'Her calling him 'Mr Aspern.''

'I don't see what that proves.'

'It proves familiarity, and familiarity implies the possession of mementoes, of tangible objects. I can't tell you how that 'Mr' affects me — how it bridges over the gulf of time and brings our hero near to me — nor what an edge it gives to my desire to see Juliana. You don't say 'Mr' Shakespeare.'

'Would I, any more, if I had a box full of his letters?'

'Yes, if he had been your lover and someone wanted them!' And I added that John Cumnor was so convinced, and so all the more convinced by Miss Bordereau's tone, that he would have come himself to Venice on the undertaking were it not for the obstacle of his having, for any confidence, to disprove his identity with the person who had written to them, which the old ladies would be sure to suspect in spite of dissimulation and a change of name. If they were to ask him point-blank if he were not their snubbed correspondent it would be too awkward for him to lie; whereas I was fortunately not tied in that way. I was a fresh hand — I could protest without lying.

'But you'll have to take a false name,' said Mrs Prest. 'Juliana lives out of the world as much as it is possible to live, but she has none the less probably heard of Mr Aspern's editors. She perhaps possesses what you've published.'

'I've thought of that,' I returned; and I drew out of my pocket-book a visiting card neatly engraved with a well-chosen *nom de guerre*.

'You're very extravagant — it adds to your immorality. You might have done it in pencil or ink,' said my companion.

'This looks more genuine.'

'Certainly you've the courage of your curiosity. But it will be awkward about your letters; they won't come to you in that mask.'

'My banker will take them in and I shall go every day to get them. It will give me a little walk.'

'Shall you depend all on that?' asked Mrs Prest. 'Aren't you coming to see me?'

'Oh, you'll have left Venice for the hot months long before there are any results. I'm prepared to roast all summer — as well as through the long hereafter perhaps you'll say! Meanwhile John Cumnor will bombard me with letters addressed, in my feigned name, to the care of the *padrona*.'

'She'll recognise his hand,' my companion suggested.

'On the envelope he can disguise it.'

'Well, you're a precious pair! Doesn't it occur to you that even if you're able to say you're not Mr Cumnor in person they may still suspect you of being his emissary?'

'Certainly, and I see only one way to parry that.'

'And what may that be?'

I hesitated for a moment. 'To make love to the niece.'

'Ah,' cried my friend, 'wait till you see her!'

2

'I must work the garden — I must work the garden,' I said to myself five minutes later and while I waited, upstairs, in the long, dusky *sala*, where the bare scagliola floor gleamed vaguely in a chink of the closed shutters. The place was impressive, yet looked somehow cold and cautious. Mrs Prest had floated away, giving me a rendezvous at the end of half an hour by some neighbouring water-steps; and I had been let into the house, after pulling the rusty bell-wire, by a small red-headed and white-faced maid-servant, who was very young and not ugly and wore clicking pattens and a shawl in the fashion of a hood. She had not contented herself with opening the door from above by the usual arrangement of a creaking pulley, though she had looked down at me first from an upper window, dropping the cautious challenge which in Italy precedes the act of admission. I was so irritated as a general thing by this survival of medieval manners, though as so fond, if yet so special, an antiquarian I suppose I ought to have liked it; but, with my resolve to be genial from the threshold at any

16

price, I took my false card out of my pocket and held it up to her smiling as if it were a magic token. It had the effect of one indeed, for it brought her, as I say, all the way down. I begged her to hand it to her mistress, having first written on it in Italian the words: 'Could you very kindly see a gentleman, a travelling American, for a moment?' The little maid wasn't hostile even that was perhaps something gained. She coloured, she smiled, and looked both frightened and pleased. I could see that my arrival was a great affair, that visits in such a house were rare, and that she was a person who would have liked a bustling place. When she pushed forward the heavy door behind me I felt my foot in the citadel and promised myself ever so firmly to keep it there. She pattered across the damp, stony lower hall and I followed her up the high staircase — stonier still, as it seemed — without an invitation. I think she had meant I should wait for her below, but such was not my idea, and I took up my station in the *sala*. She flitted, at the far end of it, into impenetrable regions, and I looked at the place with my heart beating as I had known it to do in dentists' parlours. It had a gloomy grandeur, but owed its character almost all to its noble shape and to the fine architectural doors, as high as those of grand frontages, which, leading into the various rooms, repeated themselves on either side at intervals. They were surmounted with old, faded, painted escutcheons, and here and there in the spaces between them hung brown pictures, which I noted as speciously bad, in battered and tarnished frames that were yet more desirable than the canvases themselves. With the exception of several straw-bottomed chairs that kept their backs to the wall the grand obscure vista contained little else to minister to effect. It was evidently never used save as a passage, and scantly even as that. I may add that by the time the door through which the maidservant had escaped opened again my eyes had grown used to the want of light.

I hadn't meanwhile meant by my private ejaculation that I must myself cultivate the soil of the tangled enclosure which lay beneath the windows, but the lady who came toward me from the distance over the hard, shining floor might have supposed as much from the way in which, as I went rapidly to meet her, I exclaimed, taking care to speak Italian: 'The garden, the garden — do me the pleasure to tell me if it's yours!'

She stopped short, looking at me with wonder; and then, 'Nothing here is mine,' she answered in English, coldly and sadly.

'Oh, you're English; how delightful!' I

ingenuously cried. 'But surely the garden belongs to the house.'

'Yes, but the house doesn't belong to me.' She was a long, lean, pale person, habited apparently in a dull-coloured dressing gown, and she spoke very simply and mildly. She didn't ask me to sit down, any more than years before — if she were the niece — she had asked Mrs Prest, and we stood face to face in the empty, pompous hall.

'Well, then, would you kindly tell me to whom I must address myself? I'm afraid you will think me horribly intrusive, but you know I *must* have a garden — upon my honour I must!'

Her face was not young, but it was candid; it was not fresh, but it was clear. She had large eyes which were not bright and a great deal of hair which was not 'dressed' and long fine hands which were — possibly — not clean. She clasped these members almost convulsively as, with a confused, alarmed look, she broke out: 'Oh, don't take it away from us; we like it ourselves!'

'You have the use of it then?'

'Oh, yes. If it wasn't for that — !' And she gave a wan, vague smile.

'Isn't it a luxury, precisely? That's why, intending to be in Venice some weeks, possibly all summer, and having some literary work, some reading and writing to do, so that I must be quiet and yet if possible a great deal in the open air — that's why I've felt a garden to be really indispensable. I appeal to your own experience,' I went on with as sociable a smile as I could risk. 'Now can't I look at yours?'

'I don't know, I don't understand,' the poor woman murmured, planted there and letting her weak wonder deal — helplessly enough, as I felt — with my strangeness.

'I mean only from one of those windows — such grand ones as you have here — if you'll let me open the shutters.' And I walked toward the back of the house. When I had advanced half-way I stopped and waited as in the belief she would accompany me. I had been of necessity quite abrupt, but I strove at the same time to give her the impression of extreme courtesy. 'I've looked at furnished rooms all over the place, and it seems impossible to find any with a garden attached. Naturally in a place like Venice gardens are rare. It's absurd if you like, for a man, but I can't live without flowers.'

'There are none to speak of down there.' She came nearer, as if, though she mistrusted me, I had drawn her by an invisible thread. I went on again, and she continued as she followed me: 'We've a few, but they're very common. It costs too much to cultivate them; one has to have a man.'

'Why shouldn't I be the man?' I asked. 'I'll work without wages; or rather I'll put in a gardener. You shall have the sweetest flowers in Venice.'

She protested against this with a small quaver of sound that might have been at the same time a gush of rapture for my free sketch. Then she gasped: 'We don't know you — we don't know you.'

'You know me as much as I know you; or rather much more, because you know my name. And if you're English I'm almost a countryman.'

'We're not English,' said my companion watching me in practical submission while I threw open the shutters of one of the divisions of the wide high window.

'You speak the language so beautifully: might I ask what you are?' Seen from above the garden was in truth shabby, yet I felt at a glance that it had great capabilities. She made no rejoinder, she was so lost in her blankness and gentleness, and I exclaimed: 'You don't mean to say you're also by chance American?'

'I don't know. We used to be.'

'Used to be? Surely you haven't changed?'

'It's so many years ago. We don't seem to be anything now.'

'So many years that you've been living here? Well, I don't wonder at that; it's a grand old house. I suppose you all use the garden,' I went on, 'but I assure you I shouldn't be in your way. I'd be very quiet and stay quite in one corner.'

'We all use it?' she repeated after me vaguely, not coming close to the window but looking at my shoes. She appeared to think me capable of throwing her out.

'I mean all your family — as many as you are.'

'There's only one other than me. She's very old. She never goes down.'

I feel again my thrill at this close identification of Juliana; in spite of which, however, I kept my head. 'Only one other in all this great house!' I feigned to be not only amazed but almost scandalised. 'Dear lady, you must have space then to spare!'

'To spare?' she repeated — almost as for the rich unwonted joy of her spoken words.

'Why you surely don't live (two quiet women — I see *you* are quiet, at any rate) in fifty rooms!' Then with a burst of hope and cheer I put the question straight: 'Couldn't you for a good rent *let* me two or three? That would set me up!'

I had now struck the note that translated my purpose, and I needn't reproduce the whole of the tune I played. I ended by making my entertainer believe me an undesigning person, though of course, I didn't even attempt to persuade her I was not an eccentric one. I repeated that I had studies to pursue; that I wanted quiet; that I delighted in a garden and had vainly sought one up and down the city; that I would undertake that before another month was over the dear old house should be smothered in flowers. I think it was the flowers that won my suit, for I afterwards found that Miss Tina — for such the name of this high tremulous spinster proved somewhat incongruously to be — had an insatiable appetite for them. When I speak of my suit as won I mean that before I left her she had promised me she would refer the question to her aunt. I invited information as to who her aunt might be and she answered 'Why, Miss Bordereau!' with an air of surprise, as if I might have been expected to know. There were contradictions like this in Miss Tina which, as I observed later, contributed to make her rather pleasingly incalculable and interesting. It was the study of the two ladies to live so that the world shouldn't talk of them or touch them, and yet they had never altogether accepted the idea that it didn't hear of them. In Miss Tina at any rate a grateful susceptibility to human contact had not died out, and contact of a limited order there would be if I should come to live in the house.

'We've never done anything of the sort; we've never had a lodger or any kind of inmate.' So much as this she made a point of saying to me. 'We're very poor, we live very badly — almost on nothing. The rooms are very bare — those you might take; they've nothing at all in them. I don't know how you'd sleep, how you'd eat.'

'With your permission I could easily put in a bed and a few tables and chairs. *C'est la moindre des choses* and the affair of an hour or two. I know a little man from whom I can hire for a trifle what I should so briefly want, what I should use; my gondolier can bring the things round in his boat. Of course, in this great house you must have a second kitchen, and my servant who's a wonderfully handy fellow' — this personage was an evocation of the moment — 'can easily cook me a chop there. My tastes and habits are of the simplest; I live on flowers!' And then I ventured to add that if they were very poor it was all the more reason they should let their rooms. They were bad economists — I had never heard of such a waste of material.

I saw in a moment my good lady had never before been spoken to in any such fashion

— with a humorous firmness that didn't exclude sympathy, that was quite founded on it. She might easily have told me that my sympathy was impertinent, but this by good fortune didn't occur to her. I left her with the understanding that she would submit the question to her aunt and that I might come back the next day for their decision.

'The aunt will refuse; she'll think the whole proceeding very *louche!*' Mrs Prest declared shortly after this, when I had resumed my place in her gondola. She had put the idea into my head and now — so little are women to be counted on — she appeared to take a despondent view of it. Her pessimism provoked me and I pretended to have the best hopes; I went so far as to boast of a distinct prevision of success. Upon this Mrs Prest broke out: 'Oh, I see what's in your head! You fancy you've made such an impression in five minutes that she's dying for you to come and can be depended on to bring the old one round. If you do get in you'll count it as a triumph.'

I did count it as a triumph, but only for the commentator — in the last analysis — not for the man, who had not the tradition of personal conquest. When I went back on the morrow the little maidservant conducted me straight through the long *sala* — it opened there as before in large perspective and was lighter now, which I thought a good omen — into the apartment from which the recipient of my former visit had emerged on that occasion. It was a spacious, shabby parlour with a fine old painted ceiling under which a strange figure sat alone at one of the windows. They come back to me now almost with the palpitation they caused, the successive states marking my consciousness that as the door of the room closed behind me I was really face to face with the Juliana of some of Aspern's most exquisite and most renowned lyrics. I grew used to her afterwards, though never completely; but as she sat there before me my heart beat as fast as if the miracle of resurrection had taken place for my benefit. Her presence seemed somehow to contain and express his own, and I felt nearer to him at that first moment of seeing her than I ever had been before or ever have been since. Yes, I remember my emotions in their order, even including a curious little tremor that took me when I saw the niece not to be there. With her, the day before, I had become sufficiently familiar, but it almost exceeded my courage — much as I had longed for the event — to be left alone with so terrible a relic as the aunt. She was too strange, too literally resurgent. Then came a check from the

26

perception that we weren't really face to face, inasmuch as she had over her eyes a horrible green shade which served for her almost as a mask. I believed for the instant that she had put it on expressly, so that from underneath it she might take me all in without my getting at herself. At the same time it created a presumption of some ghastly death's-head lurking behind it. The divine Juliana as a grinning skull — the vision hung there until it passed. Then it came to me that she *was* tremendously old — so old that death might take her at any moment, before I should have time to compass my end. The next thought was a correction to that; it lighted up the situation. She would die next week, she would die tomorrow — then I could pounce on her possessions and ransack her drawers. Meanwhile she sat there neither moving nor speaking. She very small and shrunken, bent forward with her hands in her lap. She was dressed in black and her head was wrapped in a piece of old black lace which showed no hair.

My emotion keeping me silent she spoke first, and the remark she made was exactly the most unexpected.

3

'Our house is very far from the centre, but the little canal is very *comme il faut.*'

'It's the sweetest corner of Venice and I can imagine nothing more charming,' I hastened to reply. The old lady's voice was very thin and weak, but it had an agreeable, cultivated murmur and there was wonder in the thought that that individual note had been in Jeffrey Aspern's ear.

'Please do sit down there. I hear very well,' she said quietly, as if perhaps I had been shouting; and the chair she pointed to was at a certain distance. I took possession of it, assuring her I was perfectly aware of my intrusion and of my not having been properly introduced, and that I could but throw myself on her indulgence. Perhaps the other lady, the one I had had the honour of seeing the day before, would have explained to her about the garden. That was literally what had given me courage to take a step so unconventional. I had fallen in love at sight with the whole place — she herself was probably so used to it that she didn't know the impression it was capable of making on a stranger — and I had felt it really a case to risk something. Was her own kindness in receiving me a sign that I was not wholly out in my calculation? It would make me extremely happy to think so. I could give her my word of honour that I was a most respectable, inoffensive person and that as a co-tenant of the palace, so to speak, they would be barely conscious of my existence. I would conform to any regulations, any restrictions, if they would only let me enjoy the garden. Moreover I should be delighted to give her references, guarantees; they would be of the very best, both in Venice and in England, as well as in America.

She listened to me in perfect stillness, and I felt her look at me with great penetration, though I could see only the lower part of her bleached and shrivelled face. Independently of the refining process of old age it had a delicacy which once must have been great. She had been very fair, she had had a wonderful complexion. She was silent a little after I had ceased speaking; then she began: 'If you're so fond of a garden why don't you go to *terra firma*, where there are so many far better than this?'

'Oh, it's the combination!' I answered, smiling; and then with rather a flight of fancy: 'It's the idea of a garden in the middle of the sea.'

'This isn't the middle of the sea; you can't so much as see the water.'

I stared a moment, wondering if she wished to convict me of fraud. 'Can't see the water? Why, dear madam, I can come up to the very gate in my boat.'

She appeared inconsequent, for she said vaguely in reply to this: 'Yes, if you've got a boat. I haven't any; it's many years since I have been in one of the *gondole*.' She uttered these words as if they designed a curious far-away craft known to her only by hearsay.

'Let me assure you of the pleasure with which I would put mine at your service!' I returned. I had scarcely said this, however, before I became aware that the speech was in questionable taste and might also do me the injury of making me appear too eager, too possessed of a hidden motive. But the old woman remained impenetrable and her attitude worried me by suggesting that she had a fuller vision of me than I had of her. She gave me no thanks for my somewhat extravagant offer, but remarked that the lady I had seen the day before was her niece; she would presently come in. She had asked her to stay away a little on purpose — had had her reasons for seeing me first alone. She relapsed into silence and I turned over the fact of these unmentioned reasons and

the question of what might come yet; also
that of whether I might venture on some
judicious remark in praise of her companion.
I went so far as to say I should be delighted to
see our absent friend again: she had been so
very patient with me, considering how odd
she must have thought me — a declaration
which drew from Miss Bordereau another of
her whimsical speeches.

'She has very good manners; I bred her up
myself!' I was on the point of saying that that
accounted for the easy grace of the niece, but
I arrested myself in time, and the next
moment the old woman went on: 'I don't
care who you may be — I don't want to
know; it signifies very little today.' This had all
the air of being a formula of dismissal, as if
her next words would be that I might take
myself off now that she had had the
amusement of looking on the face of such a
monster of indiscretion. Therefore I was all
the more surprised when she added in her
soft, venerable quaver: 'You may have as
many rooms as you like — if you'll pay me a
good deal of money.'

I hesitated but an instant, long enough to
measure what she meant in particular by this
condition. First it struck me that she must
have really a large sum in her mind; then I
reasoned quickly that her idea of a large sum

would probably not correspond to my own. My deliberation, I think, was not so visible as to diminish the promptitude with which I replied: 'I will pay with pleasure and of course in advance whatever you may think it proper to ask me.'

'Well, then, a thousand francs a month,' she said instantly, while her baffling green shade continued to cover her attitude.

The figure, as they say, was startling and my logic had been at fault. The sum she had mentioned was, by the Venetian measure of such matters, exceedingly large; there was many an old palace in an out-of-the-way corner that I might on such terms have enjoyed the whole of by the year. But so far as my resources allowed I was prepared to spend money, and my decision was quickly taken. I would pay her with a smiling face what she asked, but in that case I would make it up by getting hold of my 'spoils' for nothing. Moreover, if she had asked five times as much I should have risen to the occasion, so odious would it have seemed to me to stand chaffering with Aspern's Juliana. It was queer enough to have a question of money with her at all. I assured her that her views perfectly met my own and that on the morrow I should have the pleasure of putting three months' rent into her hand. She received this

announcement with apparent complacency
and with no discoverable sense that after all it
would become her to say that I ought to see
the rooms first. This didn't occur to her and
indeed, her serenity was mainly what I
wanted. Our little agreement was just
concluded when the door opened and the
younger lady appeared on the threshold. As
soon as Miss Bordereau saw her niece she
cried out almost gaily: 'He'll give three
thousand — three thousand tomorrow!'

Miss Tina stood still, her patient eyes
turning from one of us to the other; then she
brought out scarcely above her breath: 'Do
you mean francs?'

'Did you mean francs or dollars?' the old
woman asked of me at this.

'I think francs were what you said,' I
sturdily smiled.

'That's very good,' said Miss Tina, as if she
had felt how overreaching her own question
might have looked.

'What do *you* know? You're ignorant,' Miss
Bordereau remarked; not with acerbity but
with a strange soft coldness.

'Yes, of money — certainly of money!' Miss
Tina hastened to concede.

'I'm sure you've your own fine branches
of knowledge,' I took the liberty of saying
genially. There was something painful to me,

33

somehow, in the turn the conversation had taken, in the discussion of dollars and francs.

'She had a very good education when she was young. I looked into that myself,' said Miss Bordereau. Then she added: 'But she has learned nothing since.'

'I have always been with you,' Miss Tina rejoined very mildly, and of a certainty with no intention of an epigram.

'Yes, but for that — !' her aunt declared with more satirical force. She evidently meant that but for this her niece would never have got on at all; the point of the observation, however, being lost on Miss Tina, though she blushed at hearing her history revealed to a stranger. Miss Bordereau went on, addressing herself to me: 'And what time will you come tomorrow with the money?'

'The sooner the better. If it suits you I'll come at noon.'

'I am always here, but I have my hours,' said the old woman as if her convenience were not to be taken for granted.

'You mean the times when you receive?'

'I never receive. But I'll see you at noon, when you come with the money.'

'Very good, I shall be punctual.' To which added: 'May I shake hands with you on our contract?' I thought there ought to be some little form; it would make me really feel easier, for I was sure there would be no other. Besides, though Miss Bordereau couldn't today be called personally attractive and there was something even in her wasted antiquity that bade one stand at one's distance, I felt an irresistible desire to hold in my own for a moment the hand Jeffrey Aspern had pressed.

For a minute she made no answer, and I saw that my proposal failed to meet with her approbation. She indulged in no movement of withdrawal which I half expected: she only said coldly: 'I belong to a time when that was not the custom.'

I felt rather snubbed. I exclaimed good-humouredly to Miss Tina: 'Oh, you'll do as well!' I shook hands with her while she assented with a small flutter. 'Yes, yes, to show it's all arranged!'

'Shall you bring the money in gold?' Miss Bordereau demanded as I was turning to the door.

I looked at her a moment. 'Aren't you a little afraid, after all, of keeping such a sum as that in the house?' It was not that I was annoyed at her avidity, but was truly struck with the disparity between such a treasure and such scanty means of guarding it.

'Whom should I be afraid of if I'm not afraid of you?' she asked with her shrunken grimness.

'Ah, well,' I laughed, 'I shall be in point of fact a protector and I'll bring gold if you prefer.'

'Thank you,' the old woman returned with dignity and with an inclination of her head which evidently signified my dismissal. I passed out of the room thinking how hard it would be to circumvent her. As I stood in the *sala* again I saw that Miss Tina had followed me, and I supposed that as her aunt had neglected to suggest I should take a look at my quarters it was her purpose to repair the omission. But she made no such overture; she only stood there with a dim, though not a languid smile, and with an effect of irresponsible, incompetent youth almost comically at variance with the faded facts of her person. She was not infirm, like her aunt, but struck me as more deeply futile, because her inefficiency was inward, which was not the case with Miss Bordereau's. I waited to see if she would offer to show me the rest of the house, but I didn't precipitate the question, inasmuch as my plan was from the moment to spend as much of my time as possible in her society. A minute, indeed, elapsed before I committed myself.

'I've had better fortune than I hoped. It was very kind of her to see me. Perhaps you said a good word for me.'

'It was the idea of the money,' said Miss Tina.

'And did you suggest that?'

'I told her you'd perhaps pay largely.'

'What made you think that?'

'I told her I thought you were rich.'

'And what put that into your head?'

'I don't know; the way you talked.'

'Dear me, I must talk differently now,' I returned. 'I'm sorry to say it's not the case.'

'Well,' said Miss Tina, 'I think that in Venice the *forestieri* in general often give a great deal for something that after all isn't much.' She appeared to make this remark with a comforting intention, to wish to remind me that if I had been extravagant I wasn't foolishly singular. We walked together along the *sala*, and as I took its magnificent measure I said that I was afraid it wouldn't form part of my *quartiere* Were my rooms by chance to be among those that opened into it? 'Not if you go above — to the second floor,' she answered as if she had rather taken for granted I would know my proper place.

'And I infer that that's where your aunt would like me to be.'

'She said your apartments ought to be very distinct.'

'That certainly would be best.' And I listened with respect while she told me that above I should be free to take whatever I might like; that there was another staircase, but only from the floor on which we stood, and that to pass from it to the garden-level or to come up to my lodging I should have to cross the great hall. This was an immense point gained; I foresaw that it would constitute my whole leverage in my relations with the two ladies. When I asked Miss Tina how I was to manage at present to find my way up she replied with an access of that sociable shyness which constantly marked her manner:

'Perhaps you can't. I don't see — unless I should go with you.' She evidently hadn't thought of this before.

We ascended to the upper floor and visited a long succession of empty rooms. The best of them looked over the garden; some of the others had above the opposite rough-tiled house-tops a view of the blue lagoon. They were all dusty and even a little disfigured with long neglect, but I saw that by spending a few hundred francs I should be able to make three or four of them habitable enough. My experiment was turning out costly, yet now that I had all but taken possession I ceased to allow this to trouble me. I mentioned to my companion a few of the things I should put in, but she replied rather more precipitately than usual that I might do exactly what I liked: she seemed to wish to notify me that the Misses Bordereau would take none but the most veiled interest in my proceedings. I guessed that her aunt had instructed her to adopt this tone, and I may as well say now that I came afterwards to distinguish perfectly (as I believed) between the speeches she made on her own responsibility and those the old woman imposed upon her. She took no notice of the unswept condition of the rooms and indulged neither in explanations nor in apologies. I said to myself that this was a sign Juliana and her niece — disenchanting idea! — were untidy persons with a low Italian standard; but I afterwards recognised that a lodger who had forced an entrance had no *locus standi* as a critic. We looked out of a good many windows, for there was nothing within the rooms to look at, and still I wanted to linger. I asked her what several different objects in the prospect might be, but in no case did she appear to know. She was evidently not familiar with the view — it was as if she had not looked at it for years — and I presently saw that she was too preoccupied with something else to pretend to care for it. Suddenly she said — the remark was not suggested:

'I don't know whether it will make any

difference to you, but the money is for me.'

'The money — ?'

'The money you're going to bring.'

'Why, you'll make me wish to stay here two or three years!' I spoke as benevolently as possible, though it had begun to act on my nerves that these women so associated with Aspern should so constantly bring the pecuniary question back.

'That would be very good for me,' she answered almost gaily.

'You put me on my honour!'

She looked as if she failed to understand this, but went on: 'She wants me to have more. She thinks she's going to die.'

'Ah, not soon I hope!' I cried with genuine feeling. I had perfectly considered the possibility of her destroying her documents on the day she should feel her end at hand. I believed that she would cling to them till then, and I was as convinced of her reading Aspern's letters over every night or at least pressing them to her withered lips. I would have given a good deal for some view of these solemnities. I asked Miss Tina if her venerable relative were seriously ill, and she replied that she was only very tired — she had lived so extraordinarily long. That was what she said herself — she wanted to die for a change. Besides, all her friends had been dead for ages; either they ought to have remained or she ought to have gone. That was another thing her aunt often said: she was not at all resigned — resigned, that is, to life.

'But people don't die when they like, do they?' Miss Tina inquired. I took the liberty of asking why, if there was actually enough money to maintain both of them, there would not be more than enough in case of her being left alone. She considered this difficult problem a moment and then said: 'Oh, well, you know, she takes care of me. She thinks that when I'm alone I shall be a great fool and shan't know how to manage.'

'I should have supposed rather that you took care of *her*. I'm afraid she's very proud.'

'Why, have you discovered that already?' Miss Tina cried with a dimness of glad surprise.

'I was shut up with her there for a considerable time and she struck me, she interested me extremely. It didn't take me long to make my discovery. She won't have much to say to me while I'm here.'

'No, I don't think she will,' my companion averred.

'Do you suppose she has some suspicion of me?'

Miss Tina's honest eyes gave me no sign I had touched a mark. 'I shouldn't think so

— letting you in after all so easily.'

'You call it easily? She has covered her risk,' I said. 'But where is it one could take an advantage of her?'

'I oughtn't to tell you if I knew, ought I?' And Miss Tina added, before I had time to reply to this, smiling dolefully: 'Do you think we've any weak points?'

'That's exactly what I'm asking. You'd only have to mention them for me to respect them religiously.'

She looked at me hereupon with that air of timid but candid and even gratified curiosity with which she had confronted me from the first; after which she said: 'There's nothing to tell. We're terribly quiet. I don't know how the days pass. We've no life.'

'I wish I might think I should bring you a little.'

'Oh, we know what we want,' she went on. 'It's all right.'

There were twenty things I desired to ask her: how in the world did they live; whether they had any friends or visitors, any relations in America or in other countries. But I judged such probings premature; I must leave it to a later chance. 'Well, don't *you* be proud,' I contented myself with saying. 'Don't hide from me altogether.'

'Oh, I must stay with my aunt,' she returned

without looking at me. And at the same moment, abruptly, without any ceremony of parting, she quitted me and disappeared, leaving me to make my own way downstairs. I stayed awhile longer wandering about the bright desert — the sun was pouring in — of the old house, thinking the situation over on the spot. Not even the pattering little *serva* came to look after me, and I reflected that after all this treatment showed confidence.

4

Perhaps it did, but all the same, six weeks later, towards the middle of June, the moment when Mrs Prest undertook her annual migration, I had made no measurable advance. I was obliged to confess to her that I had no results to speak of. My first step had been unexpectedly rapid, but there was no appearance it would be followed by a second. I was a thousand miles from taking tea with my hostesses — that privilege of which, as I reminded my good friend, we both had had a vision. She reproached me with lacking boldness and I answered that even to be bold you must have an opportunity: you may push on through a breach, but you can't batter down a dead wall. She returned that the breach I had already made was big enough to admit an army and accused me of wasting precious hours in whimpering in her *salon* when I ought to have been carrying on the struggle in the field. It is true that I went to see her very often — all on the theory that it would console me (I freely expressed my discouragement) for my want of success on my own premises. But I began to feel that it

44

didn't console me to be perpetually chaffed for my scruples, especially since I was really so vigilant; and I was rather glad when my ironic friend closed her house for the summer. She had expected to gather amusement from the drama of my intercourse with the Misses Bordereau, and was disappointed that the intercourse, and consequently the drama, had not come off. 'They'll lead you on to your ruin,' she said before she left Venice. 'They'll get all your money without showing you a scrap.' I think I settled down to my business with more concentration after her departure.

It was a fact that up to that time I had not, save on a single brief occasion, had even a moment's contact with my queer hostesses. The exception had occurred when I carried them according to my promise the terrible three thousand francs. Then I found Miss Tina awaiting me in the hall, and she took the money from my hand with a promptitude that prevented my seeing her aunt. The old lady had promised to receive me, yet apparently thought nothing of breaking that vow. The money was contained in a bag of chamois leather, of respectable dimensions, which my banker had given me, and Miss Tina had to make a big fist to receive it. This she did with extreme solemnity, though I tried to treat the affair a little as a joke. It was in no jocular strain, yet it was with a clearness akin to a brightness that she inquired, weighing the money in her two palms: 'Don't you think it's too much?' To which I replied that this would depend on the amount of pleasure I should get for it. Hereupon she turned away from me quickly, as she had done the day before, murmuring in a tone different from any she had used hitherto: 'Oh, pleasure, pleasure — there's no pleasure in this house!'

After that, for a long time, I never saw her, and I wondered the common chances of the day shouldn't have helped us to meet. It could only be evident that she was immensely on her guard against them; and in addition to this the house was so big that for each other we were lost in it. I used to look out for her hopefully as I crossed the *sala* in my comings and goings, but I was not rewarded with a glimpse of the tail of her dress. It was as if she never peeped out of her aunt's apartment. I used to wonder what she did there week after week and year after year. I had never met so stiff a policy of seclusion; it was more than keeping quiet — it was like hunted creatures feigning death. The two ladies appeared to have no visitors whatever and no sort of contact with the world. I judged at least that people couldn't have come to the house and that Miss Tina couldn't have gone out without my catching some view of it. I did what I disliked myself for doing — considering it but as once in a way: I questioned my servant about their habits and let him infer that I should be interested in any information he might glean. But he gleaned amazingly little for a knowing Venetian: it must be added that where there is a perpetual fast there are very few crumbs on the floor. His ability in other ways was sufficient, if not quite all I had attributed to him on the occasion of my first interview with Miss Tina. He had helped my gondolier to bring me round a boat-load of furniture; and when these articles had been carried to the top of the palace and distributed according to our associated wisdom he organised my household with such dignity as answered to its being composed exclusively of himself. He made me in short as comfortable as I could be with my indifferent prospects. I should have been glad if he had fallen in love with Miss Bordereau's maid or, failing this, had taken her in aversion; either event might have brought about some catastrophe, and a catastrophe might have led to some parley. It was my idea that she would have been sociable, and I myself on various occasions saw her flit to and fro on domestic errands, so that I was sure she was accessible. But I tasted of no gossip from that fountain, and I afterwards learned that Pasquale's affections were fixed upon an object that made him heedless of other women. This was a young lady with a powdered face, a yellow cotton gown and much leisure, who used often to come to see him. She practised, at her convenience, the art of a stringer of beads — these ornaments are made in Venice to profusion; she had her pocket full of them and I used to find them on the floor of my apartment — and kept an eye on the possible rival in the house. It was not for me, of course, to make the domestics tattle, and I never said a word to Miss Bordereau's cook.

It struck me as a proof of the old woman's resolve to have nothing to do with me that she should never have sent me a receipt for my three months, rent. For some days I looked out for it and then, when I had given it up, wasted a good deal of time in wondering what her reason had been for neglecting so indispensable and familiar a form. At first I was tempted to send her a reminder; after which I put by the idea — against my judgement as to what was right in the particular case — on the general ground of wishing to keep quiet. If Miss

Bordereau suspected me of ulterior aims she would suspect me less if I should be businesslike, and yet I consented not to be. It was possible she intended her omission as an impertinence, a visible irony, to show how she could overreach people who attempted to overreach her. On that hypothesis it was well to let her see that one didn't notice her little tricks. The real reading of the matter, I afterwards gathered, was simply the poor lady's desire to emphasise the fact that I was in the enjoyment of a favour as rigidly limited as it had been liberally bestowed. She had given me part of her house, but she wouldn't add to that so much as a morsel of paper with her name on it. Let me say that even at first this didn't make me too miserable, for the whole situation had the charm of its oddity. I foresaw that I should have a summer after my own literary heart, and the sense of playing with my opportunity was much greater after all than any sense of being played with. There could be no Venetian business without patience, and since I adored the place I was much more in the spirit of it for having laid in a large provision. That spirit kept me perpetual company and seemed to look out at me from the revived immortal face — in which all his genius shone — of the great poet who was my prompter. I had invoked him and he had come; he hovered before me half the time; it was as if his bright ghost had returned to earth to assure me he regarded the affair as his own no less than as mine and that we should see it fraternally and fondly to a conclusion. It was as if he had said: 'Poor dear, be easy with her; she had some natural prejudices; only give her time. Strange as it may appear to you she was very attractive in 1820. Meanwhile aren't we in Venice together, and what better place is there for the meeting of dear friends? See how it glows with the advancing summer; how the sky and the sea and the rosy air and the marble of the palaces all shimmer and melt together.' My eccentric private errand became a part of the general romance and the general glory — I felt even a mystic companionship, a moral fraternity with all those who in the past had been in the service of art. They had worked for beauty, for a devotion; and what else was I doing? That element was in everything that Jeffrey Aspern had written, and I was only bringing it to light.

I lingered in the *sala* when I went to and fro; I used to watch — as long as I thought decent — the door that led to Miss Bordereau's part of the house. A person observing me might have supposed I was trying to cast a spell on it or attempting some odd experiment in hypnotism. But I was only praying it might open or thinking what treasure probably lurked behind it. I hold it singular, as I look back, that I should never have doubted for a moment that the sacred relics were there; never have failed to know the joy of being beneath the same roof with them. After all they were under my hand — they had not escaped me yet; and they made my life continuous, in a fashion, with the illustrious life they had touched at the other end. I lost myself in this satisfaction to the point of assuming — in my quiet extravagance — that poor Miss Tina also went back, and still went back, as I used to phrase it. She did indeed, the gentle spinster, but not quite so far as Jeffrey Aspern, who was simple hearsay to her quite as he was to me. Only she had lived for years with Juliana, she had seen and handled all mementoes and — even though she was stupid — some esoteric knowledge had rubbed off on her. That was what the old woman represented — esoteric knowledge; and this was the idea with which my critical heart used to thrill. It literally beat faster often, of an evening when I had been out, as I stopped with my candle in the re-echoing hall on my way up to bed. It was as if at such a moment as that, in the stillness and after the long contradiction of the day, Miss Bordereau's secrets were in the air, the wonder of her survival more vivid. These were the acute impressions. I had them in another form, with more of a certain shade of reciprocity, during the hours I sat in the garden looking up over the top of my book at the closed windows of my hostess. In these windows no sign of life ever appeared; it was as if, for fear of my catching a glimpse of them, the two ladies passed their days in the dark. But this only emphasised their having matters to conceal; which I had wished to prove. Their motionless shutters became as expressive as eyes consciously closed, and I took comfort in the probability that, though invisible themselves, they kept me in view between the lashes.

I made a point of spending as much time as possible in the garden, to justify the picture I had originally given of my horticultural passion. And I not only spent time, but (hang it! as I said) spent precious money. As soon as I had got my rooms arranged and could give the question proper thought I surveyed the place with a clever expert and made terms for having it put in order. I was sorry to do this, for personally, I liked it better as it was, with its weeds and its wild rich tangle, its sweet characteristic Venetian shabbiness. I had to be consistent, to keep my promise that I would smother the house in flowers. Moreover I clung to the fond fancy that by flowers I should make my way — I should succeed by big nosegays. I would batter the old women with lilies — I would bombard their citadel with roses. Their door would have to yield to the pressure when a mound of fragrance should be heaped against it. The place in truth had been brutally neglected. The Venetian capacity for dawdling is of the largest, and for a good many days unlimited litter was all my gardener had to show for his ministrations. There was a great digging of holes and carting about of earth, and after a while I grew so impatient that I had thoughts of sending for my 'results' to the nearest stand. But I felt sure my friends would see through the chinks of their shutters where such tribute *couldn't* have been gathered, and might so make up their minds against my veracity. I possessed my soul and finally, though the delay was long, perceived some appearances of bloom. This encouraged me and I waited serenely enough till they multiplied. Meanwhile the real summer days arrived and began to pass, and as I look back upon them they seem to me almost the happiest of my life. I took more and more care to be in the garden, whenever it was not too hot. I had an arbour arranged and a low table and an armchair put into it; and I carried out books and portfolios — I had always some business of writing in hand — and worked and waited and mused and hoped, while the golden hours elapsed and the plants drank in the light and the inscrutable old palace turned pale and then, as the day waned, began to recover and flush and my papers rustled in the wandering breeze of the Adriatic.

Considering how little satisfaction I got from it at first it is wonderful I shouldn't have grown more tired of trying to guess what mystic rites of ennui the Misses Bordereau celebrated in their darkened rooms; whether this had always been the tenor of their life and how in previous years they had escaped elbowing their neighbours. It was supposable they had then had other habits, forms, and resources; that they must once have been young or at least middle-aged. There was no end to the questions it was possible to ask about them and no end to the answers it was not possible to frame. I had known many of my country-people in Europe and was familiar with the strange ways they were liable to take up there; but the Misses Bordereau formed altogether a new type of the American absentee. Indeed, it was clear the American name had ceased to have any application to them

— I had seen this in the ten minutes spent in the old woman's room. You could never have said whence they came from the appearance of either of them; wherever it was they had long ago shed and unlearned all native marks and notes. There was nothing in them one recognised or fitted, and, putting the question of speech aside, they might have been Norwegians or Spaniards. Miss Bordereau, after all, had been in Europe nearly three-quarters of a century; it appeared by some verses addressed to her by Aspern on the occasion of his own second absence from America — verses of which Cumnor and I had after infinite conjecture established solidly enough the date — that she was even then, as a girl of twenty, on the foreign side of the sea. There was a profession in the poem — I hope not just for the phrase — that he had come back for her sake. We had no real light on her circumstances at that moment, any more than we had upon her origin, which we believed to be of the sort usually spoken of as modest. Cumnor had a theory that she had been a governess in some family in which the poet visited and that, in consequence of her position, there was from the first something unavowed, or rather something quite clandestine, in their relations. I on the other hand had hatched a little romance according to which she was the daughter of an artist, a painter or a sculptor, who had left the Western world, when the century was fresh, to study in the ancient schools. It was essential to my hypothesis that this amiable man should have lost his wife, should have been poor and unsuccessful, and should have had a second daughter of a disposition quite different from Juliana's. It was also indispensable that he should have been accompanied to Europe by these young ladies and should have established himself there for the remainder of a struggling, saddened life. There was a further implication that Miss Bordereau had had in her youth a perverse and reckless, albeit a generous and fascinating character, and that she had braved some wondrous chances. By what passions had she been ravaged, by what adventures and sufferings had she been blanched, what store of memories had she laid away for the monotonous future?

I asked myself these things as I sat spinning theories about her in my arbour and the bees droned in the flowers. It was incontestable that, whether for right or for wrong, most readers of certain of Aspern's poems (poems not as ambiguous as the sonnets — scarcely more divine, I think — of Shakespeare) had taken for granted that Juliana had not always adhered to the steep footway of renunciation. There hovered about her name a perfume of impenitent passion, an intimation that she had not been exactly as the respectable young person in general. Was this a sign that her singer had betrayed her, had given her away, as we say nowadays, to posterity? Certain it is that it would have been difficult to put one's finger on the passage in which her fair name suffered injury. Moreover, was not any fame fair enough that was so sure of duration and was associated with works immortal through their beauty? It was a part of my idea that the young lady had had a foreign lover — and say an unedifying tragical rupture — before her meeting with Jeffrey Aspern. She had lived with her father and sister in a queer, old-fashioned, expatriated, artistic Bohemia of the days when the aesthetic was only the academic and the painters who knew the best models of *contadina* and *pifferaro* wore peaked hats and long hair. It was a society less awake than the coteries of today — in its ignorance of the wonderful chances, the opportunities of the early bird, with which its path was strewn — to tatters of old stuff and fragments of old crockery; so that Miss Bordereau appeared not to have picked up or have inherited many objects of importance. There was no enviable *bric-à-brac*, with its provoking legend of cheapness, in the room in which I had seen her. Such a fact as that suggested bareness, but none the less it worked happily into the sentimental interest I had always taken in the early movement of my countrymen as visitors to Europe. When Americans went abroad in 1820 there was something romantic, almost heroic in it, as compared with the perpetual ferryings of the present hour, the hour at which photography and other conveniences have annihilated surprise. Miss Bordereau had sailed with her family on a tossing brig in the days of long voyages and sharp differences; she had had her emotions on the top of yellow diligences, passed the night at inns where she dreamed of travellers' tales, and was most struck, on reaching the Eternal City, with the elegance of Roman pearls and scarfs and mosaic brooches. There was something touching to me in all that, and my imagination frequently went back to the period. If Miss Bordereau carried it there, of course Jeffrey Aspern had at other times done so with greater force. It was a much more important fact, if one was looking at his genius critically, that he had lived in the days before the general transfusion. It had happened to me to regret that he had known Europe at all; I should have liked to see what he would have written without that experience, by which he had incontestably been enriched. But as his fate had ruled otherwise I went with him — I tried to judge how the general old order would have struck him. It was not only there, however, I watched him; the relations he had entertained with the special new had even a livelier interest. His own country after all had had most of his life, and his muse, as they said at that time, was essentially American. That was originally what I had prized him for; that at a period when our native land was nude and crude and provincial, when the famous 'atmosphere' it is supposed to lack was not even missed, when literature was lonely there and art and form almost impossible, he had found means to live and write like one of the first; to be free and general and not at all afraid; to feel, understand, and express everything.

5

I was seldom at home in the evening, for when I attempted to occupy myself in my apartments the lamplight brought in a swarm of noxious insects, and it was too hot for closed windows. Accordingly I spent the late hours either on the water — the moonlights of Venice are famous — or in the splendid square which serves as a vast forecourt to the strange old church of Saint Mark. I sat in front of Florian's café eating ices, listening to music, talking with acquaintances: the traveller will remember how the immense cluster of tables and little chairs stretches like a promontory into the smooth lake of the Piazza. The whole place, of a summer's evening, under the stars and with all the lamps, all the voices and light footsteps on marble — the only sounds of the immense arcade that encloses it — is an open-air saloon dedicated to cooling drinks and to a still finer degustation, that of the splendid impressions received during the day. When I didn't prefer to keep mine to myself there was always a stray tourist, disencumbered of his Baedeker, to discuss them with, or some domesticated painter rejoicing in the return of the season of strong effects. The great basilica, with its low domes and bristling embroideries, the mystery of its mosaic and sculpture, looked ghostly in the tempered gloom, and the sea-breeze passed between the twin columns of the Piazzetta, the lintels of a door no longer guarded, as gently as if a rich curtain swayed there. I used sometimes on these occasions to think of the Misses Bordereau and of the pity of their being shut up in apartments which in the Venetian July even Venetian vastness couldn't relieve of some stuffiness. Their life seemed miles away from the life of the Piazza, and no doubt it was really too late to make the austere Juliana change her habits. But poor Miss Tina would have enjoyed one of Florian's ices, I was sure; sometimes I even had thoughts of carrying one home to her. Fortunately my patience bore fruit and I was not obliged to do anything so ridiculous.

One evening about the middle of July I came in earlier than usual — I forget what chance had led to this — and instead of going up to my quarters made my way into the garden. The temperature was very high; it was such a night as one would gladly have spent in the open air, and I was in no hurry to go to bed. I had floated home in my gondola, listening to the slow splash of the oar in the dark, narrow canals, and now the only thought that occupied me was that it would be good to recline at one's length in the fragrant darkness on a garden bench. The odour of the canal was doubtless at the bottom of that aspiration, and the breath of the garden, as I entered it, gave consistency to my purpose. It was delicious — just such an air as must have trembled with Romeo's vows when he stood among the thick flowers and raised his arms to his mistress's balcony. I looked at the windows of the palace to see if by chance the example of Verona — Verona being not far off — had been followed; but everything was dim, as usual, and everything was still. Juliana might on the summer nights of her youth have murmured down from open windows at Jeffrey Aspern, but Miss Tina was not a poet's mistress any more than I was a poet. This, however, didn't prevent my gratification from being great as I became aware on reaching the end of the garden that my younger *padrona* was seated in one of the bowers. At first I made out but an indistinct figure, not in the least counting on such an overture from one of my hostesses; it even occurred to me that some enamoured maidservant had stolen in to keep a tryst with her sweetheart. I was going to turn away, not to frighten her, when the figure rose to its height and I recognised Miss Bordereau's niece. I must do myself the justice that I didn't wish to frighten her either, and much as I had longed for some such accident I should have been capable of retreating. It was as if I had laid a trap for her by coming home earlier than usual and by adding to that oddity my invasion of the garden. As she rose she spoke to me, and then I guessed that perhaps, secure in my almost inveterate absence, it was her nightly practice to take a lonely airing. There was no trap in truth, because I had had no suspicion. At first I took the words she uttered for an impatience of my arrival; but as she repeated them — I hadn't caught them clearly — I had the surprise of hearing her say: 'Oh, dear, I'm so glad you've come!' She and her aunt had in common the property of unexpected speeches. She came out of the arbour almost as if to throw herself in my arms.

I hasten to add that I escaped this ordeal and that she didn't even then shake hands with me. It was an ease to her to see me and presently she told me why — because she was nervous when out of doors at night alone. The plants and shrubs looked so strange in the dark, and there were all sorts of queer sounds — she couldn't tell what they were

— like the noises of animals. She stood close to me, looking about her with an air of greater security but without any demonstration of interest in me as an individual. Then I felt how little nocturnal prowlings could have been her habit, and I was also reminded — I had been afflicted by the same in talking with her before I took possession — that it was impossible to allow too much for her simplicity.

'You speak as if you were lost in the back woods,' I cheeringly laughed. 'How you manage to keep out of this charming place when you've only three steps to take to get into it is more than I've yet been able to discover. You hide away amazingly so long as I'm on the premises, I know; but I had a hope you peeped out a little at other times. You and your poor aunt are worse off than Carmelite nuns in their cells. Should you mind telling me how you exist without air, without exercise, without any sort of human contact? I don't see how you carry on the common business of life.'

She looked at me as if I had spoken a strange tongue, and her answer was so little of one that I felt it made for irritation. 'We go to bed very early — earlier than you'd believe.' I was on the point of saying that this only deepened the mystery, but she gave me some relief by adding:

'Before you came we weren't so private.

But I've never been out at night.'

'Never in these fragrant alleys, blooming here under your nose?'

'Ah,' said Miss Tina, 'they were never nice till now!' There was a finer sense in this and a flattering comparison, so that it seemed to me I had gained some advantage. As I might follow that further by establishing a good grievance I asked her why, since she thought my garden nice, she had never thanked me in any way for the flowers I had been sending up in such quantities for the previous three weeks. I had not been discouraged — there had been, as she would have observed, a daily armful; but I had been brought up in the common forms and a word of recognition now and then would have touched me in the right place.

'Why, I didn't know they were for me!'

'They were for both of you. Why should I make a difference?'

Miss Tina reflected as if she might be thinking of a reason for that, but she failed to produce one. Instead of this she asked abruptly: 'Why in the world do you want so much to know us?'

'I ought, after all, to name a difference,' I replied. 'That question's your aunt's; it isn't yours. You wouldn't ask it if you hadn't been put up to it.'

'She didn't tell me to ask you,' Miss Tina replied without confusion. She was, indeed, the oddest mixture of shyness and straightness.

'Well, she has often wondered about it herself and expressed her wonder to you. She has insisted on it, so that she had put the idea into your head that I'm insufferably pushing. Upon my word, I think I've been very discreet. And how completely your aunt must have lost every tradition of sociability, to see anything out of the way in the idea that respectable, intelligent people, living as we do under the same roof, should occasionally exchange a remark! What could be more natural? We are of the same country and have at least some of the same tastes, since, like you, I'm intensely fond of Venice.'

My friend seemed incapable of grasping more than one clause in any proposition, and she now spoke quickly, eagerly, as if she were answering my whole speech: 'I'm not in the least fond of Venice. I should like to go far away!'

'Has she always kept you back so?' I went on, to show her I could be as irrelevant as herself.

'She told me to come out tonight; she has told me very often,' said Miss Tina. 'It is I who wouldn't come. I don't like to leave her.'

'Is she too weak, is she really failing?' I demanded, with more emotion, I think, than I meant to betray. I measured this by the way her eyes rested on me in the darkness. It embarrassed me a little, and to turn the matter off I continued genially: 'Do let us sit down together comfortably somewhere — while you tell me all about her.'

Miss Tina made no resistance to this. We found a bench less secluded, less confidential, as it were, than the one in the arbour; and we were still sitting there when I heard midnight ring out from those clear bells of Venice which vibrate with a solemnity of their own over the lagoon and hold the air so much more than the chimes of other places. We were together more than an hour and our interview gave, as it struck me, a great lift to my undertaking. Miss Tina accepted the situation without a protest; she had avoided me for three months, yet now she treated me almost as if these three months had made me an old friend. If I had chosen I might have gathered from this that though she had avoided me she had given a good deal of consideration to doing so. She paid no attention to the flight of time — never worried at my keeping her so long away from her aunt. She talked freely, answering questions and asking them and not even taking advantage of certain longish pauses by which they were naturally broken to say she thought she had better go in. It was almost as if she were waiting for something — something I might say to her — and intended to give me my opportunity. I was the more struck by this as she told me how much less well her aunt had been for a good many days, and in a way that was rather new. She was markedly weaker; at moments she showed no strength at all; yet more than ever before she wished to be left alone. That was why she had told her to come out — not even to remain in her own room, which was alongside; she pronounced poor Miss Tina 'a worry, a bore, and a source of aggravation.' She sat still for hours together, as if for long sleep; she had always done that, musing and dozing; but at such times formerly she gave, in breaks, some small sign of life, of interest, liking her companion to be near her with her work. This sad personage confided to me that at present her aunt was so motionless as to create the fear she was dead; moreover, she scarce ate or drank — one couldn't see what she lived on. The great thing was that she still on most days got up; the serious job was to dress her, to wheel her out of her bedroom. She clung to as many of her old habits as possible and had always, little company as they had received for years, made a point of sitting in the great parlour.

I scarce knew what to think of all this — of Miss Tina's sudden conversion to sociability and of the strange fact that the more the old woman appeared to decline to her end the less she should desire to be looked after. The story hung indifferently together, and I even asked myself if it mightn't be a trap laid for me, the result of a design to make me show my hand. I couldn't have told why my companions (as they could only by courtesy be called) should have this purpose — why they should try to trip up so lucrative a lodger. But at any hazard I kept on my guard, so that Miss Tina shouldn't have occasion again to ask what I might really be 'up to.' Poor woman, before we parted for the night my mind was at rest as to what *she* might be. She was up to nothing at all.

She told me more about their affairs than I had hoped; there was no need to be prying, for it evidently drew her out simply to feel me listen and care. She ceased wondering why I should, and at last, while describing the brilliant life they had led years before, she almost chattered. It was Miss Tina who judged it brilliant; she said that when they first came to live in Venice, years and years back — I found her essentially vague about dates and the order in which events had occurred — there was never a week they hadn't some visitor or didn't make some pleasant *passeggio* in the town. They had seen all the curiosities; they had even been to the Lido in a boat — she spoke as if I might think there was a way on foot; they had had a collation there, brought in three baskets and spread out on the grass. I asked her what people she had known and she said, Oh, very nice ones — the Cavaliere Bombicci and the Contessa Altemura, with whom they had had a great friendship! Also English people — the Churtons and the Goldies and Mrs Stock-Stock, whom they had loved dearly; she was dead and gone, poor dear. That was the case with most of their kind circle — this expression was Miss Tina's own; though a few were left, which was a wonder, considering how they had neglected them. She mentioned the names of two or three Venetian old women; of a certain doctor, very clever, who was so attentive — he came as a friend, he had really given up practice; of the *avvocato* Pochintesta, who wrote beautiful poems and had addressed one to her aunt. These people came to see them without fail every year, usually at the *capo d'anno*, and of old her aunt used to make them some little present — her aunt and she together: small things that she, Miss Tina turned out with her own hand, paper lampshades, or mats for the decanters of wine at dinner, or those woollen things that in cold weather are worn on the wrists. The last few years there hadn't been many presents; she couldn't think what to make and her aunt had lost interest and never suggested. But the people came all the same; if the good Venetians liked you once they liked you for ever.

There was affecting matter enough in the good faith of this sketch of former social glories; the picnic at the Lido had remained vivid through the ages and poor Miss Tina evidently was of the impression that she had had a dashing youth. She had in fact had a glimpse of the Venetian world in its gossiping, home-keeping, parsimonious professional walks; for I noted for the first time how nearly she had acquired by contact the trick of the familiar soft-sounding, almost infantile prattle of the place. I judged her to have imbibed this invertebrate dialect from the natural way the names of things and people — most purely local — rose to her lips. If she knew little of what they represented she knew still less of anything else. Her aunt had drawn in — the failure of interest in the table-mats and lamp-shades was a sign of that — and she hadn't been able to mingle in society or to entertain it alone; so that her range of reminiscence

71

struck one as an old world altogether. Her tone, hadn't it been so decent, would have seemed to carry one back to the queer rococo Venice of Goldoni and Casanova. I found myself mistakenly thinking of her, too, as one of Jeffrey Aspern's contemporaries; this came from her having so little in common with my own. It was possible, I indeed reasoned, that she hadn't even heard of him; it might very well be that Juliana had forborne to lift for innocent eyes the veil that covered the temple of her glory. In this case she perhaps wouldn't know of the existence of the papers, and I welcomed that presumption — it made me feel more safe with her — till I remembered we had believed the letter of disavowal received by Cumnor to be in the handwriting of the niece. If it had been dictated to her she had of course to know what it was about; though the effect of it withal was to repudiate the idea of any connection with the poet. I held it probable, at all events, that Miss Tina hadn't read a word of his poetry. Moreover if, with her companion, she had always escaped invasion and research, there was little occasion for her having got it into her head that people were 'after' the letters. People had not been after them, for people hadn't heard of them. Cumnor's fruitless feeler would have been a solitary accident.

When midnight sounded Miss Tina got up; but she stopped at the door of the house only after she had wandered two or three times with me round the garden. 'When shall I see you again?' I asked before she went in; to which she replied with promptness that she should like to come out the next night. She added, however, that she shouldn't come — she was so far from doing everything she liked.

'You might do a few things *I* like,' I quite sincerely sighed.

'Oh, you — I don't believe you!' she murmured at this, facing me with her simple solemnity.

'Why don't you believe me?'

'Because I don't understand you.'

'That's just the sort of occasion to have faith.' I couldn't say more, though I should have liked to, as I saw I only mystified her; for I had no wish to have it on my conscience that I might pass for having made love to her. Nothing less should I have seemed to do had I continued to beg a lady to 'believe in me' in an Italian garden on a midsummer night. There was some merit in my scruples, for Miss Tina lingered and lingered: I made out in her the conviction that she shouldn't really soon come down again and the wish, therefore, to protract the present. She insisted, too, on making the talk between us personal to ourselves; and altogether her behaviour was such as would have been possible only to a perfectly artless and a considerably witless woman.

'I shall like the flowers better now that I know them also meant for me.'

'How could you have doubted it? If you'll tell me the kind you like best I'll send a double lot.'

'Oh, I like them all best!' Then she went on familiarly: 'Shall you study — shall you read and write — when you go up to your rooms?'

'I don't do that at night — at this season. The lamplight brings in the animals.'

'You might have known that when you came.'

'I did know it!'

'And in winter do you work at night?'

'I read a good deal, but I don't often write.' She listened as if these details had a rare interest, and suddenly a temptation quite at odds with all the prudence I had been teaching myself glimmered at me in her plain, mild face. Ah, yes, she was safe and I could make her safer! It seemed to me from one moment to another that I couldn't wait longer — that I really must take a sounding. So I went on: 'In general before I go to sleep (very often in bed; it's a bad habit, but I confess to it) I read some great poet. In nine cases out of ten it's a volume of Jeffrey Aspern.'

I watched her well as I pronounced that name, but I saw nothing wonderful. Why should I, indeed? Wasn't Jeffrey Aspern the property of the human race?

'Oh, *we* read him — we *have* read him,' she quietly replied.

'He's my poet of poets — I know him almost by heart.'

For an instant Miss Tina hesitated; then her sociability was too much for her. 'Oh, by heart — that's nothing'; and, though dimly, she quite lighted. 'My aunt used to know him — to know him' — she paused an instant and I wondered what she was going to say — 'to know him as a visitor.'

'As a visitor?' I guarded my tone.

'He used to call on her and take her out.'

I continued to stare. 'My dear lady, he died a hundred years ago!'

'Well,' she said amusingly, 'my aunt's a hundred and fifty.'

'Mercy on us!' I cried; 'why didn't you tell me before? I should like so to ask her about him.'

'She wouldn't care for that — she wouldn't tell you,' Miss Tina returned.

'I don't care what she cares for! She *must*

tell me — it's not a chance to be lost.'

'Oh, you should have come twenty years ago. Then she still talked about him.'

'And what did she say?' I eagerly asked.

'I don't know — that he liked her immensely.'

'And she — didn't she like *him*?'

'She said he was a god.' Miss Tina gave me this information flatly, without expression; her tone might have made it a piece of trivial gossip. But it stirred me deeply as she dropped the words into the summer night; their sound might have been the light rustle of an old unfolded love-letter.

'Fancy, fancy!' I murmured. And then: 'Tell me this, please — has she got a portrait of him? They're distressingly rare.'

'A portrait? I don't know,' said Miss Tina; and now there was discomfiture in her face. 'Well, good-night!' she added; and she turned into the house.

I accompanied her into the wide, dusky, stone paved passage that corresponded on the ground floor with our grand *sala*. It opened at one end into the garden, at the other upon the canal, and was lighted now only by the small lamp always left for me to take up as I went to bed. An extinguished candle which Miss Tina apparently had brought down with her stood on the same table with it.

'Good-night, good-night!' I replied, keeping beside her as she went to get her light. 'Surely you'd know, shouldn't you, if she had one?'

'If she had what?' the poor lady asked, looking at me queerly over the flame of her candle.

'A portrait of the god. I don't know what I wouldn't give to see it.'

'I don't know what she has got. She keeps her things locked up.' And Miss Tina went away toward the staircase with the sense evidently of having said too much.

I let her go — I wished not to frighten her — and I contented myself with remarking that Miss Bordereau wouldn't have locked up such a glorious possession as that: a thing a person would be proud of and hang up in a prominent place on the parlour-wall. Therefore of course she hadn't any portrait. Miss Tina made no direct answer to this and, candle in hand, with her back to me mounted two or three degrees. Then she stopped short and turned round, looking at me across the dusky space.

'Do you write — do you write?' There was a shake in her voice — she could scarcely bring it out.

'Do I write? Oh, don't speak of my writing on the same day with Aspern's!'

'Do you write about *him* — do you pry into his life?'

'Ah, that's your aunt's question; it can't be yours!' I said in a tone of slightly wounded sensibility.

'All the more reason, then, that you should answer it. Do you, please?'

I thought I had allowed for the falsehoods I should have to tell, but I found that in fact when it came to the point I hadn't. Besides, now that I had an opening there was a kind of relief in being frank. Lastly — it was perhaps fanciful, even fatuous — I guessed that Miss Tina personally wouldn't in the last resort be less my friend. So after a moment's hesitation I answered: 'Yes, I've written about him and I'm looking for more material. In heaven's name have you got any?'

'*Santo Dio!*' she exclaimed, without heeding my question; and she hurried upstairs and out of sight. I might count upon her in the last resort, but for the present she was visibly alarmed. The proof of it was that she began to hide again, so that for a fortnight I kept missing her. I found my patience ebbing, and after four or five days of this I told the gardener to stop the 'floral tributes.'

6

One afternoon, at last however, as I came down from my quarters to go out, I found her in the *sala*; it was our first encounter on that ground since I had come into the house. She put on no air of being there by accident; there was an ignorance of such arts in her honest, angular diffidence. That I might be quite sure she was waiting for me she mentioned it at once, but telling me with it that Miss Bordereau wished to see me: she would take me into the room at that moment if I had time. If I had been late for a love-tryst I would have stayed for this, and I quickly signified that I should be delighted to wait on my benefactress. 'She wants to talk with you — to know you,' Miss Tina said, smiling as if she herself appreciated that idea; and she led me to the door of her aunt's apartment. I stopped her a moment before she had opened it, looking at her with some curiosity. I told her that this was a great satisfaction to me and a great honour; but all the same I should like to ask what had made Miss Bordereau so markedly and suddenly change. It had been only the other day that she wouldn't suffer me near her. Miss Tina was not embarrassed by my question; she had as many little unexpected serenities, plausibilities, almost, as if she told fibs, but the odd part of them was that they had on the contrary their source in her truthfulness. 'Oh, my aunt varies', she answered; 'it's so terribly dull — suppose she's tired.'

'But you told me she wanted more and more to be alone.'

Poor Miss Tina coloured as if she found me too pushing. 'Well, if you don't believe she wants to see you, I haven't invented it! I think people often are capricious when they're very old.'

'That's perfectly true. I only wanted to be clear as to whether you've repeated to her what I told you the other night.'

'What you told me!'

'About Jeffrey Aspern — that I'm looking for materials.'

'If I had told her, do you think she'd have sent for you?'

'That's exactly what I want to know. If she wants to keep him to herself she might have sent for me to tell me so.'

'She won't speak of him,' said Miss Tina. Then as she opened the door she added in a lower tone: 'I told her nothing.'

The old woman was sitting in the same

place in which I had seen her last, in the same position, with the same mystifying bandage over her eyes. Her welcome was to turn her almost invisible face to me and show me that while she sat silent she saw me clearly. I made no motion to shake hands with her; I now felt too well that this was out of place for ever. It had been sufficiently enjoined — too venerable to touch. There was something so grim in her aspect — it was partly the accident of her green shade — as I stood there to be measured, that I ceased on the spot to doubt her suspecting me, though I didn't in the least myself suspect that Miss Tina hadn't betrayed me, but the old woman's brooding instinct had served her; she had turned me over and over in the long, still hours and had guessed. The worst of it was that she looked terribly like an old woman who at a pinch would, even like Sardanapalus, burn her treasure. Miss Tina pushed a chair forward, saying to me: 'This will be a good place for you to sit.' As I took possession of it I asked after Miss Bordereau's health; expressed the hope that in spite of the very hot weather it was satisfactory. She answered that it was good enough — good enough; that it was a great thing to be alive.

'Oh, as to that, it depends upon what you

compare it with!' I returned with a laugh.

'I don't compare — I don't compare. If I did that I should have given everything up long ago.'

I liked to take this for a subtle allusion to the rapture she had known in the society of Jeffrey Aspern — though it was true that such an allusion would have accorded ill with the wish I imputed to her to keep him buried in her soul. What it accorded with was my constant conviction that no human being had ever had a happier social gift than his, and what it seemed to convey was that nothing in the world was worth speaking of if one pretended to speak of that. But one didn't pretend! Miss Tina sat down beside her aunt, looking as if she had reason to believe some wonderful talk would come off between us.

'It's about the beautiful flowers,' said the old lady; 'you sent us so many — I ought to have thanked you for them before. But I don't write letters and I receive company but at long intervals.'

She hadn't thanked me while the flowers continued to come, but she departed from her custom so far as to send for me as soon as she began to fear they wouldn't come any more. I noted this; I remembered what an acquisitive propensity she had shown me when it was a question of extracting gold from me, and I privately rejoiced at the happy thought I had had in suspending my tribute. She had missed it and was willing to make a concession to bring it back. At the first sign of this concession could only go to meet her. 'I'm afraid you haven't had many, of late, but they shall begin again immediately — tomorrow, tonight.'

'Oh, do send us some tonight!' Miss Tina cried as if it were a great affair.

'What else should you do with them? It isn't a manly taste to make a bower of your room,' the old woman remarked.

'I don't make a bower of my room, but I'm exceedingly fond of growing flowers, of watching their ways. There's nothing unmanly in that: it has been the amusement of philosophers, of statesmen in retirement; even, I think, of great captains.'

'I suppose you know you can sell them — those you don't use,' Miss Bordereau went on. 'I dare say they wouldn't give you much for them; still, you could make a bargain.'

'Oh, I've never in my life made a bargain, as you ought pretty well to have gathered. My gardener disposes of them and I ask no questions.'

'I'd ask a few, I can promise you!' said Miss Bordereau; and it was so I first heard the strange sound of her laugh, which was as if the faint 'walking' ghost of her old-time tone had suddenly cut a caper. I couldn't get used to the idea that this vision of pecuniary profit was most what drew out the divine Juliana.

'Come into the garden yourself and pick them; come as often as you like; come every day. The flowers are all for you,' I pursued, addressing Miss Tina and carrying off this veracious statement by treating it as an innocent joke. 'I can't imagine why she doesn't come down,' I added for Miss Bordereau's benefit.

'You must make her come; you must come up and fetch her,' the old woman said to my satisfaction. 'That odd thing you've made in the corner will do very well for her to sit in.'

The allusion to the most elaborate of my shady coverts, a sketchy 'summer-house,' was irreverent; it confirmed the impression I had already received that there was a flicker of impertinence in Miss Bordereau's talk, a vague echo of the boldness or the archness of her adventurous youth and which had somehow automatically outlived passions and faculties. None the less, I asked: 'Wouldn't it be possible for you to come down there yourself? Wouldn't it do you good to sit there in the shade and the sweet air?'

'Oh, sir, when I move out of this it won't be to sit in the air, and I'm afraid that any that may be stirring around me won't be particularly sweet! It will be a very dark shade indeed. But that won't be just yet,' Miss Bordereau continued cannily, as if to correct any hopes this free glance at the last receptacle of her mortality might lead me to entertain. 'I've sat here many a day and have had enough of arbours in my time. But I'm not afraid to wait till I'm called.'

Miss Tina had expected, as I felt, rare conversation, but perhaps she found it less gracious on her aunt's side — considering I had been sent for with a civil intention — than she had hoped. As to give the position a turn that would put our companion in a light more favourable she said to me: 'Didn't I tell you the other night that she had sent me out? You see I can do what I like!'

'Do you pity her — do you teach her to pity herself?' Miss Bordereau demanded, before I had time to answer this appeal. 'She has a much easier life than I had at her age.'

'You must remember it has been quite open to me,' I said, 'to think you rather inhuman.'

'Inhuman? That's what the poets used to call the women a hundred years ago. Don't try that; you won't do as well as they!' Juliana went on. 'There's no more poetry in the world — that I know of, at least. But I won't bandy words with you,' she said, and I well

85

remember the old-fashioned, artificial sound she gave the speech. 'You make me talk, talk, talk! It isn't good for me at all.' I got up at this and told her I would take no more of her time; but she detained me to put a question: 'Do you remember, the day I saw you about the rooms, that you offered us the use of your gondola?' And when I assented, promptly struck again with her disposition to make a 'good thing' of my being there and wondering what she now had in her eye, she produced: 'Why don't you take that girl out in it and show her the place?'

'Oh, dear aunt, what do you want to do with me?' cried the 'girl,' with a piteous quaver. 'I know all about the place!'

'Well, then, go with him and explain!' said Miss Bordereau, who gave an effect of cruelty to her implacable power of retort. This showed her as a sarcastic, profane, cynical old woman. 'Haven't we heard that there have been all sorts of changes in all these years? You ought to see them, and at your age — I don't mean because you're so young — you ought to take the chances that come. You're old enough, my dear, and this gentleman won't hurt you. He'll show you the famous sunsets, if they still go on — *do* they go on? The sun set for me so long ago. But that's not a reason. Besides, I shall never miss you; you

86

think you're too important. Take her to the Piazza; it used to be very pretty,' Miss Bordereau continued, addressing herself to me. 'What have they done with the funny old church? I hope it hasn't tumbled down. Let her look at the shops; she may take some money, she may buy what she likes.'

Poor Miss Tina had got up, discountenanced and helpless, and as we stood there before her aunt it would certainly have struck a spectator of the scene that our venerable friend was making rare sport of us. Miss Tina protested in a confusion of exclamations and murmurs; but I lost no time in saying that if she would do me the honour to accept the hospitality of my boat I would engage she really shouldn't be bored. Or if she didn't want so much of my company, the boat itself, with the gondolier, was at her service; he was a capital oar and she might have every confidence. Miss Tina, without definitely answering this speech, looked away from me and out of the window quite as if about to weep, and I remarked that once we had Miss Bordereau's approval we could easily come to an understanding. We would take an hour, whichever she liked, one of the very next days. As I made my obeisance to the old lady I asked her if she would kindly permit me to see her again.

For a moment she kept me; then she said: 'Is it very necessary to your happiness?'

'It diverts me more than I can say.'

'You're wonderfully civil. Don't you know it almost kills *me*?'

'How can I believe that when I see you more animated, more brilliant than when I came in?'

'That's very true, aunt,' said Miss Tina. 'I think it does you good.'

'Isn't it touching, the solicitude we each have that the other shall enjoy himself?' sneered Miss Bordereau. 'If you think me brilliant today you don't know what you are talking about; you've never seen an agreeable woman. What do you people know about good society?' she cried; but before I could tell her, 'Don't try to pay me a compliment; I've been spoiled,' she went on. 'My door's shut, but you may sometimes knock.'

With this she dismissed me and I left the room. The latch closed behind me, but Miss Tina, contrary to my hope, had remained within. I passed slowly across the hall and, before taking my way downstairs waited a little. My hope was answered; after a minute my conductress followed me. 'That's a delightful idea about the Piazza', I said. 'When will you go — tonight, tomorrow?'

She had been disconcerted, as I have

mentioned, but I had already perceived, and I was to observe again, that when Miss Tina was embarrassed she didn't — as most women would have in like case — turn away, floundering and hedging, but came closer, as it were, with a deprecating, a clinging appeal to be spared, to be protected. Her attitude was a constant prayer for aid and explanation, and yet no woman in the world could have been less of a comedian. From the moment you were kind to her she depended on you absolutely; her self-consciousness dropped and she took the greatest intimacy, the innocent intimacy that was all she could conceive, for granted. She didn't know, she now declared, what possessed her aunt, who had changed so quickly, who had got some idea. I replied that she must catch the idea and let me have it: we would go and take an ice together at Florian's and she should report while we listened to the band.

'Oh, it will take me a long time to be able to 'report'!' she said rather ruefully; and she could promise me this satisfaction neither for that night nor for the next. I was patient now, however, for I felt I had only to wait; and in fact at the end of the week, one lovely evening after dinner, she stepped into my gondola, to which in honour of the occasion I had attached a second oar.

We swept in the course of five minutes into the Grand Canal; whereupon she uttered a murmur of ecstasy as fresh as if she had been a tourist just arrived. She had forgotten the splendour of the great waterway on a clear summer evening, and how the sense of floating between marble palaces and reflected lights disposed the mind to freedom and ease. We floated long and far, and though my friend gave no high-pitched voice to her glee I was sure of her full surrender. She was more than pleased, she was transported; the whole thing was an immense liberation. The gondola moved with slow strokes, to give her time to enjoy it, and she listened to the plash of the oars, which grew louder and more musically liquid as we passed into narrow canals, as if it were a revelation of Venice. When I asked her how long it was since she had thus floated, she answered: 'Oh, I don't know; a long time — not since my aunt began to be ill.' This was not the only show of her extreme vagueness about the previous years and the line marking off the period of Miss Bordereau's eminence. I was not at liberty to keep her out long, but we took a considerable *giro* before going to the Piazza. I asked her no questions, holding off by design from her life at home and the things I wanted to know. I poured, rather, treasures of information about

90

the objects before and around us into her ears, describing also Florence and Rome, discoursing on the charms and advantages of travel. She reclined, receptive, on the deep leather cushion, turned her eyes conscientiously to everything I noted and never mentioned to me till some time afterwards that she might be supposed to know Florence better than I, as she had lived there for years with her kinswoman. At last she said with the shy impatience of a child: 'Are we not really going to the Piazza? That's what I want to see!' I immediately gave the order that we should go straight, after which we sat silent with the expectation of arrival. As some time still passed, however, she broke out of her own movement: 'I've found out what's the matter with my aunt: she's afraid you'll go!'

I quite gasped. 'What has put that into her head?'

'She has had an idea you've not been happy. That's why she is different now.'

'You mean, she wants to make me happier?'

'Well, she wants you not to go. She wants you to stay.'

'I suppose you mean on account of the rent,' I remarked candidly.

Miss Tina's candour but profited. 'Yes, you know; so that I shall have more.'

'How much does she want you to have?' I asked with all the gaiety I now felt. 'She ought to fix the sum, so that I may stay till it's made up.'

'Oh, that wouldn't please me,' said Miss Tina. 'It would be unheard of, your taking that trouble.'

'But suppose I should have my own reasons for staying in Venice?'

'Then it would be better for you to stay in some other house.'

'And what would your aunt say to that?'

'She wouldn't like it at all. But I should think you'd do well to give up your reasons and go away altogether.'

'Dear Miss Tina,' I said, 'it's not so easy to give up my reasons!'

She made no immediate answer to this, but after a moment broke out afresh: 'I think I know what your reasons are!'

'I dare say, because the other night I almost told you how I wished you'd help me to make them good.'

'I can't do that without being false to my aunt.'

'What do you mean by being false to her?'

'Why, she would never consent to what you want. She has been asked, she has been written to. It makes her fearfully angry.'

'Then she *has* papers of value?' I

precipitately cried.

'Oh, she has everything!' sighed Miss Tina, with a curious weariness, a sudden lapse into gloom.

These words caused all my pulses to throb, for I regarded them as precious evidence. I felt them too deeply to speak, and in the interval the gondola approached the Piazzetta. After we had disembarked I asked my companion if she would rather walk round the square or go and sit before the great cafe; to which she replied that she would do whichever I liked best — I must only remember again how little time she had. I assured her there was plenty to do both, and we made the circuit of the long arcades. Her spirits revived at the sight of the bright shop-windows, and she lingered and stopped, admiring or disapproving of their contents, asking me what I thought of things, theorising about prices. My attention wandered from her; her words of a while before, 'Oh, she has everything!' echoed so in my consciousness. We sat down at last in the crowded circle at Florian's, finding an unoccupied table among those that were ranged in the square. It was a splendid night and all the world out of doors; Miss Tina couldn't have wished the elements more auspicious for her return to society. I saw she felt it all even more than she told, but her impressions were well nigh too many for her. She had forgotten the attraction of the world and was learning that she had for the best years of her life been rather mercilessly cheated of it. This didn't make her angry; but as she took in the charming scene her face had, in spite of its smile of appreciation, the flush of a wounded surprise. She didn't speak, sunk in the sense of opportunities, for ever lost, that ought to have been easy; and this gave me a chance to say to her: 'Did you mean a while ago, that your aunt has a plan of keeping me on by admitting me occasionally to her presence?'

'She thinks it will make a difference with you if you sometimes see her. She wants you so much to stay that she's willing to make that concession.'

'And what good does she consider I think it will do me to see her?'

'I don't know; it must be interesting,' said Miss Tina simply. 'You told her you found it so.'

'So I did; but every one doesn't think that.'

'No, of course not, or more people would try.'

'Well, if she's capable of making that reflection she's capable also of making this further one,' I went on: 'that I must have a particular reason for not doing as others do, in spite of the interest she offers — for not leaving her alone.' Miss Tina looked as if she failed to grasp this rather complicated proposition; so I continued: 'If you've not told her what I said to you the other night may she not at least have guessed it?'

'I don't know — she's very suspicious.'

'But she hasn't been made so by indiscreet curiosity, by persecution?'

'No, no; it isn't that,' said Miss Tina, turning on me a troubled face. 'I don't know how to say it; it's on account of something — ages ago, before I was born — in her life.'

'Something? What sort of thing?' — I asked it as if I could have no idea.

'Oh, she has never told me.' And I was sure my friend spoke the truth. Her extreme limpidity was almost provoking, and I felt for the moment that she would have been more satisfactory if she had been less ingenuous. 'Do you suppose it's something to which Jeffrey Aspern's letters and papers — I mean the things in her possession — have reference?'

'I dare say it is!' my companion exclaimed as if this were a very happy suggestion. 'I've never looked at any of those things.'

'None of them? Then how do you know what they are?'

'I don't,' said Miss Tina placidly. 'I've never

had them in my hands. But I've seen them when she has had them out.'

'Does she have them out often?'

'Not now, but she used to. She's very fond of them.'

'In spite of their being compromising?'

'Compromising?' Miss Tina repeated as if vague to what that meant. I felt almost as one who corrupts the innocence of youth.

'I allude to their containing painful memories.'

'Oh, I don't think anything's painful.'

'You mean there's nothing to affect her reputation?' An odder look even than usual came at this into the face of Miss Bordereau's niece — a confession, it seemed, of helplessness, an appeal to me to deal fairly, generously with her. I had brought her to the Piazza, placed her among charming influences, paid her an attention she appreciated, and now I appeared to show it all as a bribe — a bribe to make her turn in some way against her aunt. She was of a yielding nature and capable of doing almost anything to please a person markedly kind to her; but the greatest kindness of all would be not to presume too much on this. It was strange enough as I afterwards thought, that she had not the least air of resenting my want of consideration for her aunt's character, which would have been in the worst possible taste if anything less vital — from my point of view — had been at stake. I don't think she really measured it. 'Do you mean she ever did something bad?' she asked in a moment.

'Heaven forbid I should say so, and it's none of my business. Besides, if she did,' I agreeably put it, 'that was in other ages, in another world. But why shouldn't she destroy her papers?'

'Oh, she loves them too much.'

'Even now, when she may be near her end?'

'Perhaps when she's sure of that she will.'

'Well, Miss Tina', I said, 'that's just what I should like you to prevent.'

'How can I prevent it?'

'Couldn't you get them away from her?'

'And give them to you?'

This put the case, superficially, with sharp irony, but I was sure of her not intending that. 'Oh I mean that you might let me see them and look them over. It isn't for myself, or that I should want them at any cost to any one else. It's simply that they would be of such immense interest to the public, such immeasurable importance as a contribution to Jeffrey Aspern's history.'

She listened to me in her usual way, as if I abounded in matters she had never heard of, and I felt almost as base as the reporter of a newspaper who forces his way into a house of mourning. This was marked when she presently said: 'There was a gentleman who some time ago wrote to her in very much those words. He also wanted her papers.'

'And did she answer him?' I asked, rather ashamed of not having my friend's rectitude.

'Only when he had written two or three times. He made her very angry.'

'And what did she say?'

'She said he was a devil,' Miss Tina replied categorically.

'She used that expression in her letter?'

'Oh, no; she said it to me. She made me write to him.'

'And what did you say?'

'I told him there were no papers at all.'

'Ah, poor gentleman!' I groaned.

'I knew there were, but I wrote what she bade me.'

'Of course, you had to do that. But I hope I shan't pass for a devil.'

'It will depend upon what you ask me to do for you,' my companion smiled.

'Oh, if there's a chance of *your* thinking so my affair's in a bad way! I shan't ask you to steal for me, nor even to fib — for you *can't* fib, unless on paper. But the principal thing is this — to prevent her destroying the papers.'

'Why, I've no control of her,' said Miss

Tina. 'It's she who controls me.'

'But she doesn't control her own arms and legs, does she? The way she would naturally destroy her letters would be to burn them. Now she can't burn them without fire, and she can't get fire unless you give it to her.'

'I've always done everything she has asked,' my poor friend pleaded. 'Besides, there's Olimpia.'

I was on the point of saying that Olimpia was probably corruptible, but I thought it best not to sound that note. So I simply put it that this frail creature might perhaps be managed.

'Every one can be managed by my aunt,' said Miss Tina. And then she remembered that her holiday was over; she must go home.

I laid my hand on her arm, across the table, to stay her a moment. 'What I want of you is a general promise to help me.'

'Oh, how *can* I, how *can* I?' she asked, wondering and troubled. She was half-surprised, half-frightened at my attaching that importance to her, at my calling on her for action.

'This is the main thing: to watch our friend carefully and warn me in time, before she commits that dreadful sacrilege.'

'I can't watch her when she makes me go out.'

'That's very true.'

'And when you do too.'

'Mercy on us — do you think she'll have done anything tonight?'

'I don't know. She's very cunning.'

'Are you trying to frighten me?' I asked.

I felt this question sufficiently answered when my companion murmured in a musing, almost envious way: 'Oh, but she loves them — she loves them!'

This reflection, repeated with such emphasis, gave me great comfort; but to obtain more of that balm I said: 'If she shouldn't intend to destroy the objects we speak of before her death she'll probably have made some disposition by will.'

'By will?'

'Hasn't she made a will for your benefit?'

'Ah, she has so little to leave. That's why she likes money,' said Miss Tina.

'Might I ask, since we're really talking things over, what you and she live on?'

'On some money that comes from America, from a gentleman — I think a lawyer — in New York. He sends it every quarter. It isn't much!'

'And won't she have disposed of that?'

My companion hesitated — I saw she was blushing.

'I believe it's mine,' she said; and the look

and tone which accompanied these words betrayed so the absence of the habit of thinking of herself that I almost thought her charming. The next instant she added: 'But she had in an *avvocato* here once, ever so long ago. And some people came and signed something.'

'They were probably witnesses. And you weren't asked to sign? Well then,' I argued, rapidly and hopefully, 'it's because you're the legatee. She must have left all her documents to you!'

'If she has it's with very strict conditions,' Miss Tina responded, rising quickly, while the movement gave the words a small character of decision. They seemed to imply that the bequest would be accompanied with a proviso that the articles bequeathed should remain concealed from every inquisitive eye, and that I was very much mistaken if I thought her the person to depart from an injunction so absolute.

'Oh, of course, you'll have to abide by the terms,' I said; and she uttered nothing to mitigate the rigour of this conclusion. None the less, later on, just before we disembarked at her own door after a return which had taken place almost in silence, she said to me abruptly: 'I'll do what I can to help you.' I was grateful for this — it was very well so far as it went; but it didn't keep me from remembering that night in a worried waking hour that I now had her word for it to re-enforce my own impression that the old woman was full of craft.

7

The fear of what this side of her character might have led her to do made me nervous for days afterwards. I waited for an intimation from Miss Tina; I almost read it as her duty to keep me informed, to let me know definitely whether or no Miss Bordereau had sacrificed her treasures. But as she gave no sign I lost patience and determined to put the case to the very touch of my own senses. I sent late one afternoon to ask if I might pay the ladies a visit, and my servant came back with surprising news. Miss Bordereau could be approached without the least difficulty; she had been moved out into the *sala* and was sitting by the window that overlooked the garden. I descended and found this picture correct; the old lady had been wheeled forth into the world and had a certain air, which came mainly perhaps from some brighter element in her dress, of being prepared again to have converse with it. It had not yet, however, begun to flock about her; she was perfectly alone and, though the door stood open, I had at first no glimpse of Miss Tina. The window at which she sat had the afternoon shade and, one of the shutters having been pushed back, she could see the pleasant garden, where the summer sun had by this time dried up too many of the plants — she could see the yellow light and the long shadows.

'Have you come to tell me you'll take the rooms for six months more?' she asked as I approached her, startling me by something coarse in her cupidity almost as much as if she hadn't already given me a specimen of it. Juliana's desire to make our acquaintance lucrative had been, as I have sufficiently indicated, a false note in my image of the woman who had inspired a great poet with immortal lines; but I may say here definitely that I after all recognised large allowance to be made for her. It was I who had kindled the unholy flame; it was I who had put into her head that she had the means of making money. She appeared never to have thought of that; she had been living wastefully for years, in a house five times too big for her, on a footing that I could explain only by the presumption that, excessive as it was, the space she enjoyed cost her next to nothing and that, small as were her revenues, they left her, for Venice, an appreciable margin. I had descended on her one day and taught her to calculate, and my almost extravagant comedy on the subject of the garden had presented me irresistibly in the light of a victim. Like all persons who achieve the miracle of changing their point of view late in life, she had been intensely converted; she had seized my hint with a desperate, tremulous clutch.

I invited myself to go and get one of the chairs that stood, at a distance, against the wall — she had given herself no concern as to whether I should sit or stand; and while I placed it near her I began gaily: 'Oh, dear madam, what an imagination you have, what an intellectual sweep! I'm a poor devil of a man of letters who lives from day to day. How can I take palaces by the year? My existence is precarious. I don't know whether six months hence I shall have bread to put in my mouth. I've treated myself for once; it has been an immense luxury. But when it comes to going on — !'

'Are your rooms too dear? If they are you can have more for the same money,' Juliana responded. 'We can arrange, we can *combinare*, as they say here.'

'Well, yes, since you ask me, they're too dear, much too dear,' I said. 'Evidently you suppose me richer than I am.'

She looked at me as from the mouth of her cave. 'If you write books don't you sell them?'

'Do you mean don't people buy them? A

little, a very little — not so much as I could wish. Writing books, unless one be a great genius — and even then! — is the last road to fortune. I think there's no more money to be made by good letters.'

'Perhaps you don't choose nice subjects. What do you write about?' Miss Bordereau implacably pursued.

'About the books of other people. I'm a critic, a commentator, an historian, in a small way.' I wondered what she was coming to.

'And what other people now?'

'Oh, better ones than myself: the great writers mainly — the great philosophers and poets of the past; those who are dead and gone and can't, poor darlings, speak for themselves.'

'And what do you say about them?'

'I say they sometimes attached themselves to very clever women!' I replied as for pleasantness. I had measured, as I thought, my risk, but as my words fell upon the air they were to strike me as imprudent. However, I had launched them and I wasn't sorry, for perhaps after all the old woman would be willing to treat. It seemed tolerably obvious that she knew my secret; why, therefore, drag the process out? But she didn't take what I had said as a confession; she only asked:

'Do you think it's right to rake up the past?'

'I don't feel that I know what you mean by raking it up. How can we get at it unless we dig a little? The present has such a rough way of treading it down.'

'Oh, I like the past, but I don't like critics,' my hostess declared with her hard complacency.

'Neither do I, but I like their discoveries.'

'Aren't they mostly lies?'

'The lies are what they sometimes discover,' I said, smiling at the quiet impertinence of this. 'They often lay bare the truth.'

'The truth is God's, it isn't man's; we had better leave it alone. Who can judge of it? — who can say?'

'We're terribly in the dark, I know,' I admitted; 'but if we give up trying what becomes of all the fine things? What becomes of the work I just mentioned, that of the great philosophers and poets? It's all vain words if there's nothing to measure it by.'

'You talk as if you were a tailor,' said Miss Bordereau whimsically; and then she added quickly and in a different manner: 'This house is very fine; the proportions are magnificent. Today I wanted to look at this part again. I made them bring me out here. When your man came just now to learn if I would see you

I was on the point of sending for you to ask if you didn't mean to go on. I wanted to judge what I'm letting you have. This *sala* is very grand,' she pursued like an auctioneer, moving a little, as I guessed, her invisible eyes. 'I don't believe you often have lived in such a house, eh?'

'I can't afford to!' I said.

'Well, then, how much will you give me for six months?'

I was on the point of exclaiming — and the air of excruciation in my face would have denoted a moral fact — 'Don't, Juliana; for *his* sake, don't!' But I controlled myself and asked less passionately: 'Why should I remain so long as that?'

'I thought you liked it,' said Miss Bordereau, with her shrivelled dignity.

'So I thought I should.'

For a moment she said nothing more, and I left my own words to suggest to her what they might. I half expected her to say, coldly enough, that if I had been disappointed we needn't continue the discussion, and this in spite of the fact that I believed her now to have in her mind — however it had come there — what would have told her that my disappointment was natural. But to my extreme surprise she ended by observing: 'If you don't think we've treated you well enough perhaps we can discover some way of treating you better.' This speech was somehow so incongruous that it made me laugh again, and I excused myself by saying that she talked as if I were a sulky boy pouting in the corner and having to be 'brought round.' I hadn't a grain of complaint to make; and could anything have exceeded Miss Tina's graciousness in accompanying me a few nights before to the Piazza? At this the old woman went on: 'Well, you brought it on yourself!' And then in a different tone: 'She's a very fine girl.' I assented cordially to this proposition, and she expressed the hope that I did so not merely to be obliging, but that I really liked her. Meanwhile I wondered still more what Miss Bordereau was coming to. 'Except for me, today,' she said, 'she hasn't a relation in the world.' Did she, by describing her niece as amiable and unencumbered, wish to represent her as a *parti*?

It was perfectly true that I couldn't afford to go on with my rooms at a fancy price and that I had already devoted to my undertaking almost all the hard cash I had set apart for it. My patience and my time were by no means exhausted, but I should be able to draw upon them only on a more usual Venetian basis. I was willing to pay the precious personage with whom my pecuniary dealings were such a discord twice as much as any other *padrona di casa* would have asked, but I wasn't willing to pay her twenty times as much. I told her so plainly, and my plainness appeared to have some success, for she exclaimed: 'Very good; you've done what I asked you — you've made an offer!'

'Yes, but not for half a year. Only by the month.'

'Oh, I must think of that, then.' She seemed disappointed that I wouldn't tie myself to a period, and I guessed that she wished both to secure me and to discourage me; to say severely: 'Do you dream that you can get off with less than six months? Do you dream that even by the end of that time you'll be appreciably nearer your victory?' What was most in my mind was that she had a fancy to play me the trick of making me engage myself when in fact she had sacrificed her treasure. There was a moment when my suspense on the point was so acute that I all but broke out with the question, and what kept it back was but an instinctive recoil — lest it should be a mistake — from the last violence of self-exposure. She was such a subtle old witch that one could never tell where one stood with her. You may imagine whether it cleared up the puzzle when, just after she had said she would think of my proposal and without any formal transition, she drew out of her pocket with an embarrassed hand a small object wrapped in a crumpled white paper. She held it there a moment and then resumed: 'Do you know much about curiosities?'

'About curiosities?'

'About antiquities, the old gimcracks that people pay so much for today. Do you know the kind of price they bring?'

I thought I saw what was coming, but I said ingenuously: 'Do you want to buy something?'

'No, I want to sell. What would an amateur give me for that?' She unfolded the white paper and made a motion for me to take from her a small oval portrait. I possessed myself of it with fingers of which I could only hope that they didn't betray the intensity of their clutch, and she added: 'I would part with it only for a good price.'

At the first glance I recognised Jeffrey Aspern, and was well aware that I flushed with the act. As she was watching me, however, I had the consistency to exclaim: 'What a striking face! Do tell me who it is.'

'He's an old friend of mine, a very distinguished man in his day. He gave it me himself, but I'm afraid to mention his name, lest you never should have heard of him, critic and historian as you are. I know the world goes fast and one generation forgets another. He was all the fashion when I was young.'

She was perhaps amazed at my assurance, but I was surprised at hers; at her having the energy, in her state of health and at her time of life, to wish to sport with me to that tune simply for her private entertainment — the humour to test me and practise on me and befool me. This at least was the interpretation that I put upon her production of the relic, for I couldn't believe she really desired to sell it or cared for any information I might give her. What she wished was to dangle it before my eyes and put a prohibitive price on it. 'The face comes back to me, it torments me,' I said, turning the object this way and that and looking at it very critically. It was a careful but not a supreme work of art, larger than the ordinary miniature and representing a young man with a remarkably handsome face, in a high-collared green coat and a buff waistcoat. I felt in the little work a virtue of likeness and judged it to have been painted when the model was about twenty-five. There are, as all the world knows, three other portraits of the poet in existence, but none of so early a date as this elegant image. 'I've never seen the original, clearly a man of a past age, but I've seen other reproductions of this face,' I went on. 'You expressed doubt of this generation's having heard of the gentleman, but he strikes me for all the world as a celebrity. Now who is he? I can't put my finger on him — I can't give him a label. Wasn't he a writer? Surely, he's a poet.' I was determined that it should be she, not I, who should first pronounce Jeffrey Aspern's name.

My resolution was taken in ignorance of Miss Bordereau's extremely resolute character, and her lips never formed in my hearing the syllables that meant so much for her. She neglected to answer my question, but raised her hand to take back the picture, using a gesture which though impotent was in a high degree peremptory. 'It's only a person who should know for himself that would give me my price,' she said with a certain dryness.

'Oh, then you have a price?' I didn't restore the charming thing; not from any vindictive purpose, but because I instinctively clung to it. We looked at each other hard while I retained it.

'I know the least I would take. What it occurred to me to ask you about is the most I shall be able to get.'

She made a movement, drawing herself together as if, in a spasm of dread at having lost her prize, she had been impelled to the immense effort of rising to snatch it from me.

I instantly placed it in her hand again, saying as I did so: 'I should like to have it myself, but with your ideas it would be quite beyond my mark.'

She turned the small oval plate over in her lap, with its face down, and I heard her catch her breath as after a strain or an escape. This, however, did not prevent her saying in a moment: 'You'd buy a likeness of a person you don't know by an artist who has no reputation?'

'The artist may have no reputation, but that thing's wonderfully well painted,' I replied, to give myself a reason.

'It's lucky you thought of saying that, because the painter was my father.'

'That makes the picture indeed precious!' returned with gaiety; and I may add that a part of my cheer came from this proof I had been right in my theory of Miss Bordereau's origin. Aspern had, of course, met the young lady on his going to her father's studio as a sitter. I observed to Miss Bordereau that if she would entrust me with her property for twenty-four hours I should be happy to take advice on it; but she made no other reply than to slip it in silence into her pocket. This convinced me still more that she had no sincere intention of selling it during her lifetime, though she may have desired to satisfy herself as to the sum her niece, should she leave it to her, might expect eventually to obtain for it. 'Well, at any rate, I hope you won't offer it without giving me notice,' I said as she remained irresponsive. 'Remember me as a possible purchaser.'

'I should want your money first!' she returned with unexpected rudeness; and then, as if she bethought herself that I might well complain of such a tone and wished to turn the matter off, asked abruptly what I talked about with her niece when I went out with her that way of an evening.

'You speak as if we had set up the habit,' I replied. 'Certainly I should be very glad if it were to become our pleasant custom. But in that case I should feel a still greater scruple at betraying a lady's confidence.'

'Her confidence? Has my niece confidence?'

'Here she is — she can tell you herself,' I said; for Miss Tina now appeared on the threshold of the old woman's parlour. 'Have you confidence, Miss Tina? Your aunt wants very much to know.'

'Not in her, not in her!' the younger lady declared, shaking her head with a dolefulness that was neither jocular nor affected. 'I don't know what to do with her; she has fits of horrid imprudence. She's so easily tired — and yet she has begun to roam, to drag herself about the house.' And she looked down at her yoke-fellow of long years with a vacancy of wonder, as if all their contact and custom hadn't made her perversities, on occasion, any more easy to follow.'

'I know what I'm about. I'm not losing my mind. I dare say you'd like to think so,' said Miss Bordereau with a crudity of cynicism.

'I don't suppose you came out here yourself. Miss Tina must have had to lend you a hand,' I interposed for conciliation.

'Oh, she insisted we should push her; and when she insists!' said Miss Tina, in the same tone of apprehension; as if there were no knowing what service she disapproved of her aunt might force her next to render.

'I've always got most things done I wanted, thank God! The people I've lived with have humoured me,' the old woman continued, speaking out of the white ashes of her vanity.

I took it pleasantly up. 'I suppose you mean they've obeyed you.'

'Well, whatever it is — when they like one.'

'It's just because I like you that I want to resist,' said Miss Tina with a nervous laugh.

'Oh, I expect you'll bring Miss Bordereau upstairs next to pay me a visit,' I went on; to which the old lady replied:

'Oh, no; I can keep an eye on you from here!'

'You're very tired; you'll certainly be ill tonight!' cried Miss Tina.

'Nonsense, dear; I feel better at this moment than I've done for a month. Tomorrow I shall come out again. I want to be where I can see this clever gentleman.'

'Shouldn't you perhaps see me better in your sitting-room?' I asked.

'Don't you mean shouldn't you have a better chance at me?' she returned, fixing me a moment with her green shade.

'Ah, I haven't that anywhere! I look at you but don't see you.'

'You agitate her dreadfully — and that's not good,' said Miss Tina, giving me a reproachful, deterrent headshake.

'I want to watch you — I want to watch you!' Miss Bordereau went on.

'Well, then, let us spend as much of our time together as possible — I don't care where. That will give you every facility.'

'Oh, I've seen you enough for today. I'm satisfied. Now I'll go home,' Juliana said. Miss Tina laid her hands on the back of the wheeled chair and began to push, but I begged her to let me take her place. 'Oh, yes, you may move me this way — you shan't in any other!' the old woman cried as she felt herself propelled firmly and easily over the smooth, hard floor. Before we reached the door of her own apartment she bade me stop, and she took a long last look up and down the noble *sala*. 'Oh, it's a prodigious house!' she murmured; after which I pushed her forward. When we had entered the parlour Miss Tina let me know she should now be able to manage, and at the same moment the little red-haired *donna* came to meet her mistress. Miss Tina's idea was evidently to get her aunt immediately back to bed. I confess that in spite of this urgency I was guilty of the indiscretion of lingering; it held me there to feel myself so close to the objects I coveted — which would be probably put away somewhere in the faded unsociable room. The place had indeed a bareness that suggested no hidden values; there were neither dusky nooks nor curtained corners, neither massive cabinets nor chests with iron bands. Moreover it was possible, it was perhaps even likely, that the old lady had consigned her relics to her bedroom, to some battered box that was shoved under the bed, to the drawer of some lame dressing-table, where they would be in the range of vision by the dim night-lamp. None the less I turned an eye on every article of furniture, on every conceivable cover for a hoard, and noticed that there were half a dozen things with drawers, and in particular a tall old secretary with brass ornaments of the style of the Empire — a receptacle somewhat infirm but still capable of keeping rare secrets. I don't know why this article so engaged me, small purpose as I had of breaking into it; but I stared at it so hard that Miss Tina noticed me and changed colour. Her doing this made me think I was right and that, wherever they might have been before, the Aspern papers at that moment languished behind the peevish little lock of the secretary. It was hard to turn my attention from the dull mahogany front when I reflected that a plain panel divided me from the goal of my hopes; but I gathered up my slightly scattered prudence and with an effort took leave of my hostess. To make the effort graceful I said to her that I should certainly bring her an opinion about the little picture.

'The little picture?' Miss Tina asked in surprise.

'What do *you* know about it, my dear?' the old woman demanded. 'You needn't mind. I've fixed my price.'

'And what may that be?'

'A thousand pounds.'

'Oh, Lord!' cried poor Miss Tina irrepressibly.

'Is that what she talks to you about?' said Miss Bordereau.

'Imagine your aunt's wanting to know!' I had to separate from my younger friend with only those words, though I should have liked immensely to add: 'For heaven's sake meet me tonight in the garden!'

8

As it turned out, the precaution had not been needed, for three hours later, just as I had finished my dinner, Miss Tina appeared, unannounced, in the open doorway of the room in which my simple repasts were served. I remember well that I felt no surprise at seeing her; which is not a proof of my not believing in her timidity. It was immense, but in a case in which there was a particular reason for boldness it never would have prevented her from running up to my floor. I saw that she was now quite full of a particular reason; it threw her forward — made her seize me, as I rose to meet her, by the arm.

'My aunt's very ill; I think she's dying!'

'Never in the world,' I answered bitterly. 'Don't you be afraid!'

'Do go for a doctor — do, do! Olimpia's gone for the one we always have, but she doesn't come back; I don't know what has happened to her. I told her that if he wasn't at home she was to follow him where he had gone; but apparently she's following him all over Venice. I don't know what to do — she looks as if she were sinking.'

'May I see her, may I judge?' I asked. 'Of course I shall be delighted to bring someone; but hadn't we better send my man instead, so that I may stay with you?'

Miss Tina assented to this and I dispatched my servant for the best doctor in the neighbourhood. I hurried downstairs with her, and on the way she told me than an hour after I quitted them in the afternoon Miss Bordereau had had an attack of 'oppression,' a terrible difficulty in breathing. This had subsided, but had left her so exhausted that she didn't come up: she seemed all spent and gone. I repeated that she wasn't gone, that she wouldn't go yet; whereupon Miss Tina gave me a sharper sidelong glance than she had ever favoured me withal and said: 'Really, what do you mean? I suppose you don't accuse her of making-believe!' I forget what reply I made to this, but I fear that in my heart I thought the old woman capable of any weird manoeuvre. Miss Tina wanted to know what I had done to her; her aunt had told her I had made her so angry. I declared I had done nothing whatever — I had been exceedingly careful; to which my companion rejoined that our friend had assured her she had had a scene with me — a scene that had upset her. I answered with some resentment that the scene had been of *her* making — that

I couldn't think what she was angry with me for unless for not seeing my way to give a thousand pounds for the portrait of Jeffrey Aspern. 'And did she show you that? Oh, gracious — oh, deary me!' groaned Miss Tina, who seemed to feel the situation pass out of her control and the elements of her fate thicken round her. I answered her I'd give anything to possess it, yet that I had no thousand pounds; but I stopped when we came to the door of Miss Bordereau's room. I had an immense curiosity to pass it, but I thought it my duty to represent to Miss Tina that if I made the invalid angry she ought perhaps to be spared the sight of me. 'The sight of you? Do you think she can *see*?' my companion demanded, almost with indignation. I did think so but forbore to say it, and I softly followed my conductress.

I remember that what I said to her as I stood for a moment beside the old woman's bed was: 'Does she never show you her eyes, then? Have you never seen them?' Miss Bordereau had been divested of her green shade, but — it was not my fortune to behold Juliana in her nightcap — the upper half of her face was covered by the fall of a piece of dingy lacelike muslin, a sort of extemporised hood which, wound round her head, descended to the end of her nose, leaving nothing visible but her white, withered cheeks and puckered mouth, closed tightly and, as it were, consciously. Miss Tina gave me a glance of surprise, evidently not seeing a reason for my impatience. 'You mean she always wears something? She does it to preserve them.'

'Because they're so fine?'

'Oh, today, today!' And Miss Tina shook her head, speaking very low. 'But they used to be magnificent!'

'Yes, indeed — we've Aspern's word for that.' And as I looked again at the old woman's wrappings I could imagine her not having wished to allow any supposition that the great poet had overdone it. But I didn't waste my time in considering Juliana, in whom the appearance of respiration was so slight as to suggest that no human attention could ever help her more. I turned my eyes once more all over the room, rummaging with them the closets the chests of drawers, the tables. Miss Tina at once noted their direction and read, I think, what was in them; but she didn't answer it, turning away restlessly, anxiously, so that I felt rebuked, with reason, for an appetite wellnigh indecent in the presence of our dying companion. All the same, I took another view, endeavouring to pick out mentally the receptacle to try first, for a person who should wish to put his hand on Miss Bordereau's papers directly after her death. The place was a dire confusion; it looked like the dressing-room of an old actress. There were clothes hanging over chairs, odd-looking shabby bundles here and there, and various paste-board boxes piled together battered, bulging, and discoloured, which might have been fifty years old. Miss Tina after a moment noticed the direction of my eyes again, and, as if she guessed how I judged such appearances — forgetting I had no business to judge them at all — said, perhaps to defend herself from the imputation of complicity in the disorder:

'She likes it this way; we can't move things. There are old bandboxes she has had most of her life.' Then she added, half-taking pity on my real thought: 'Those things were *there*.' And she pointed to a small, low trunk which stood under a sofa that just allowed room for it. It struck me as a queer, superannuated coffer, of painted wood, with elaborate handles and shrivelled straps and with the colour — it had last been endued with a coat of light green — much rubbed off. It evidently had travelled with Juliana in the olden time — in the days of her adventures, which it had shared. It would have made a strange figure arriving at a modern hotel.

'*Were* there — they aren't now?' I asked,

startled by Miss Tina's implication.

She was going to answer, but at that moment the doctor came in — the doctor whom the little maid had been sent to fetch and whom she had at last overtaken. My servant, going on his own errand, had met her with her companion in tow, and in the sociable Venetian spirit, retracing his steps with them, had also come up to the threshold of the *padrona's* room, where I saw him peep over the doctor's shoulder. I motioned him away the more instantly that the sight of his prying face reminded me how little I myself had to do there — an admonition confirmed by the sharp way the little doctor eyed me, his air of taking me for a rival who had the field before him. He was a short, fat, brisk gentleman who wore the tall hat of his profession and seemed to look at everything but his patient. He kept me still in range, as if it struck him I too should be better for a dose, so that I bowed to him and left him with the women, going down to smoke a cigar in the garden. I was nervous; I couldn't go further; I couldn't leave the place. I don't know exactly what I thought might happen, but I felt it important to be there. I wandered about the alleys — the warm night had come on — smoking cigar after cigar and studying the light in Miss Bordereau's windows. They

126

were open now, I could see; the situation was different. Sometimes the light moved, but not quickly; it didn't suggest the hurry of a crisis. Was the old woman dying or was she already dead? Had the doctor said that there was nothing to be done at her tremendous age but to let her quietly pass away? or had he simply announced with a look a little more conventional that the end of the end had come? Were the other two women just going and coming over the offices that follow in such a case? It made me uneasy not to be nearer as if I thought the doctor himself might carry away the papers with him. I bit my cigar hard while it assailed me again that perhaps there were now no papers to carry!

I wandered about an hour and more. I looked out for Miss Tina at one of the windows, having a vague idea that she might come there to give me some sign. Wouldn't she see the red tip of my cigar in the dark and feel sure I was hanging on to know what the doctor had said? I'm afraid it's a proof of the grossness of my anxieties that I should have taken in some degree for granted at such an hour in the midst of the greatest change that could fall on her, poor Miss Tina's having also a free mind for them. My servant came down and spoke to me; he knew nothing save that the doctor had gone after a visit of half an hour. If he had stayed half an hour then Miss Bordereau was still alive: it couldn't have taken so long to attest her decease. I sent the man out of the house; there were moments when the sense of his curiosity annoyed me, and this was one of them. *He* had been watching my cigar-tip from an upper window, if Miss Tina hadn't; he couldn't know what I was after and I couldn't tell him, though I suspected in him fantastic private theories about me which he thought fine and which had I more exactly known them, I should have thought offensive.

I went upstairs at last, but I mounted no higher than the *sala*. The door of Miss Bordereau's apartment was open, showing from the parlour the dimness of a poor candle. I went towards it with a light tread, and at the same moment Miss Tina appeared and stood looking at me as I approached 'She's better, she's better,' she said even before I had asked. 'The doctor has given her something; she woke up, came back to life while he was there. He says there's no immediate danger.'

'No immediate danger? Surely he thinks her condition serious!'

'Yes, because she had been excited. That affects her dreadfully.'

'It will do so again then, because she works herself up. She did so this afternoon.'

'Yes, she mustn't come out any more,' said Miss Tina with one of her lapses into a deeper detachment.

'What's the use of making such a remark as that,' I permitted myself to ask, 'if you begin to rattle her about again the first time she bids you?'

'I won't — I won't do it any more.'

'You must learn to resist her,' I went on.

'Oh, yes, I shall; I shall do so better if you tell me it's right.'

'You mustn't do it for me — you must do it for yourself. It all comes back to you, if you're scared and upset.'

'Well, I'm not upset now,' said Miss Tina placidly enough. 'She's very quiet.'

'Is she conscious again — does she speak?'

'No, she doesn't speak, but she takes my hand. She holds it fast.'

'Yes,' I returned, 'I can see what force she still has by the way she grabbed that picture this afternoon. But if she holds you fast how comes it that you're here?'

Miss Tina waited a little; though her face was in deep shadow — she had her back to the light in the parlour and I had put down my own candle far off, near the door of the sala — I thought I saw her smile ingenuously. 'I came on purpose — I had heard your step.'

'Why, I came on tiptoe, as soundlessly as possible.'

'Well, I had heard you,' said Miss Tina.

'And is your aunt alone now?'

'Oh, no — Olimpia sits there.'

On my side I debated. 'Shall we then pass in there?' And I nodded at the parlour; I wanted more and more to be on the spot.

'We can't talk there — she'll hear us.'

I was on the point of replying that in that case we'd sit silent, but I felt too much this wouldn't do, there was something I desired so immensely to ask her. Thus I hinted we might walk a little in the *sala*, keeping more at the other end, where we shouldn't disturb our friend. Miss Tina assented unconditionally; the doctor was coming again, she said, and she would be there to meet him at the door. We strolled through the fine superfluous hall, where on the marble floor — particularly as at first we said nothing — our footsteps were more audible than I had expected. When we reached the other end — the wide window, inveterately closed, connecting with the balcony that overhung the canal — I submitted that we had best remain there, as she would see the doctor arrive the sooner. I opened the window and we passed out on the balcony. The air of the canal seemed even heavier, hotter than that of the *sala*. The place was hushed and void; the quiet neighbourhood had gone to sleep. A lamp, here and there, over the narrow black water glimmered in double; the voice of a man going homeward singing, his jacket on his shoulder and his hat on his ear, came to us from a distance. This didn't prevent the scene from being very *comme il faut*, as Miss Bordereau had called it the first time I saw her. Presently a gondola passed along the canal with its slow, rhythmical splash, and as we listened we watched it in silence. It didn't stop, it didn't carry the doctor; and after it had gone on I said to Miss Tina:

'And where are they now — the things that were in the trunk?'

'In the trunk?'

'That green box you pointed out to me in her room. You said her papers had been there; you seemed to mean she had transferred them.'

'Oh, yes; they're not in the trunk,' said Miss Tina.

'May I ask if you've looked?'

'Yes, I've looked — for you.'

'How for me, dear Miss Tina? Do you mean you'd have given them to me if you had found them?' — and I fairly trembled with the question.

She delayed to reply and I waited. Suddenly she broke out: 'I don't know what I'd do — what I wouldn't!'

'Would you look again — somewhere else?'

She had spoken with a strange, unexpected

emotion, and she went on in the same tone: 'I can't — I can't — while she lies there. It isn't decent.'

'No, it isn't decent,' I replied gravely. 'Let the poor lady rest in peace.' And the words on my lips were not hypocritical, for I felt reprimanded and shamed.

Miss Tina added in a moment, as if she had guessed this and were sorry for me, but at the same time wished to explain that I did push her, or at least harp on the chord, too much: 'I can't deceive her that way. I can't deceive her — perhaps on her death-bed.'

'Heaven forbid I should ask you, though I've been guilty myself!'

'You've been guilty?'

'I've sailed under false colours.' I felt now I must make a clean breast of it, must tell her I had given her an invented name on account of my fear her aunt would have heard of me and so refuse to take me in. I explained this as well as that I had really been a party to the letter addressed them by John Cumnor months before.

She listened with great attention, almost in fact gaping for wonder, and when I had made my confession she said: 'Then your real name — what is it?' She repeated it over twice when I had told her, accompanying it with the exclamation: 'Gracious, gracious!' Then she added: 'I like your own best.'

'So do I' — and I felt my laugh rueful. 'Ouf! it's a relief to get rid of the other.'

'So it was a regular plot — a kind of conspiracy?'

'Oh, a conspiracy — we were only two,' I replied, leaving out, of course, Mrs Prest.

She considered; I thought she was perhaps going to pronounce us very base. But this was not her way, and she remarked after a moment, as in candid, impartial contemplation: 'How much you must want them!'

'Oh, I do, passionately!' I grinned, I fear to admit. And this chance made me go on, forgetting my compunction of a moment before. 'How can she possibly have changed their place herself? How can she walk? How can she arrive at that sort of muscular exertion? How can she lift and carry things?'

'Oh, when one wants and when one has so much will!' said Miss Tina as if she had thought over my question already herself and had simply had no choice but that answer — the idea that in the dead of night, or at some moment when the coast was clear, the old woman had been capable of a miraculous effort.

'Have you questioned Olimpia? Hasn't she helped her — hasn't she done it for her?' I asked; to which my friend replied promptly and positively that their servant had had nothing to do with the matter, though without admitting definitely that she had spoken to her. It was as if she were a little shy, a little ashamed now, of letting me see how much she had entered into my uneasiness and had me on her mind. Suddenly she said to me without any immediate relevance:

'I rather feel you a new person, you know, now that you've a new name.'

'It isn't a new one; it's a very good old one, thank fortune!'

She looked at me a moment. 'Well, I do like it better.'

'Oh, if you didn't I would almost go on with the other!'

'Would you really?'

I laughed again, but I returned for an answer: 'Of course if she can rummage about that way she can perfectly have burnt them.'

'You must wait — you must wait,' Miss Tina mournfully moralised; and her tone ministered little to my patience, for it seemed, after all, to accept that wretched possibility. I would teach myself to wait, I declared nevertheless; because in the first place I couldn't do otherwise, and in the second I had her promise, given me the other night, that she would help me.

'Of course if the papers are gone that's no

use,' she said; not as if she wished to recede, but only to be conscientious.

'Naturally. But if you could only find out!' I groaned, quivering again.

'I thought you promised you'd wait.'

'Oh, you mean wait even for that?'

'For what, then?'

'Ah, nothing,' I answered rather foolishly, being ashamed to tell her what had been implied in my acceptance of delay — the idea that she would perhaps do more for me than merely find out.

I know not if she guessed this; at all events she seemed to bethink herself of some propriety of showing me more rigour. 'I didn't promise to deceive, did I? I don't think I did.'

'It doesn't much matter whether you did or not, for you couldn't!'

Nothing is more possible than that she wouldn't have contested this even hadn't she been diverted by our seeing the doctor's gondola shoot into the little canal and approach the house. I noted that he came as fast as if he believed our proprietress still in danger. We looked down at him while he disembarked and then went back into the *sala* to meet him. When he came up, however, I naturally left Miss Tina to go off with him alone, only asking her leave to come back later for news.

I went out of the house and walked far, as

far as the Piazza, where my restlessness declined to quit me. I was unable to sit down; it was very late now though there were people still at the little table in front of the cafés: I could but uneasily revolve, and I did so half a dozen times. The only comfort, none the less, was in my having told Miss Tina who I really was. At last I took my way home again, getting gradually and all but inextricably lost, as I did whenever I went out in Venice: so that it was considerably past midnight when I reached my door. The *sala* upstairs was as dark as usual, and my lamp as I crossed it found nothing satisfactory to show me. I was disappointed, for I had notified Miss Tina that I would come back for a report, and I thought she might have left a light there as a sign. The door of the ladies' apartment was closed; which seemed a hint that my faltering friend had gone to bed in impatience of waiting for me. I stood in the middle of the place, considering, hoping she would hear me and perhaps peep out, saying to myself too that she would never go to bed with her aunt in a state so critical; she would sit up and watch — she would be in a chair, in her dressing-gown. I went nearer the door; I stopped there and listened. I heard nothing at all, and at last I tapped gently. No answer came, and after another minute I turned the handle. There was no light in the room; this ought to have prevented my entrance, but it had no such effect. If I have frankly stated the importunities, the indelicacies of which my desire to possess myself of Jeffrey Aspern's papers had made me capable I needn't shrink, it seems to me, from confessing this last indiscretion. I regard it as the worst thing I did, yet there were extenuating circumstances. I was deeply though doubtless not disinterestedly anxious for more news of Juliana, and Miss Tina had accepted from me, as it were, a rendezvous which it might have been a point of honour with me to keep. It may be objected that her leaving the place dark was a positive sign that she released me, and to this I can only reply that I wished not to be released.

The door of Miss Bordereau's room was open and I could see beyond it the faintness of a taper. There was no sound — my footstep caused no one to stir. I came further into the room; I lingered there, lamp in hand. I wanted to give Miss Tina a chance to come to me if, as I couldn't doubt, she were still with her aunt. I made no noise to call her; I only waited to see if she wouldn't notice my light. She didn't, and I explained this — I found afterwards I was right — by the idea that she had fallen asleep. If she had fallen asleep her aunt was not on her mind, and my explanation ought to have led me to go out as I had come. I must repeat again that it didn't, for I found myself at the same moment given up to something else. I had no definite purpose, no bad intention, but felt myself held to the spot by an acute, though absurd, sense of opportunity. Opportunity for what I couldn't have said, inasmuch as it wasn't in my mind that I might proceed to thievery. Even had this tempted me I was confronted with the evident fact that Miss Bordereau didn't leave her secretary, her cupboard, and the drawers of her table gaping. I had no keys, no tools, and no ambition to smash her furniture. None the less it came to me that I was now, perhaps alone, unmolested, at the hour of freedom and safety, nearer to the source of my hopes than I had ever been. I held up my lamp, let the light play on the different objects as if it could tell me something. Still there came no movement from the other room. If Miss Tina was sleeping she was sleeping sound. Was she doing so — generous creature — on purpose to leave me the field? Did she know I was there and was she just keeping quiet to see what I would do — what I *could* do? Yet might I, when it came to that? She herself knew even better than how little.

I stopped in front of the secretary, gaping at it vainly and no doubt grotesquely; for what had it to say to me after all? In the first place it was locked, and in the second it almost surely contained nothing in which I was interested. Ten to one the papers had been destroyed, and even if they hadn't the keen old woman wouldn't have put them in such a place as that after removing them from the green trunk — wouldn't have transferred them, with the idea of their safety on her brain, from the better hiding-place to the worse. The secretary was more conspicuous, more exposed in a room in which she could no longer mount guard. It opened with a key, but there was a small brass handle, like a button as well, I saw this as I played my lamp over it. I did something more for the climax of my crisis; I caught a glimpse of the possibility that Miss Tina wished me really to understand. If she didn't so wish me, if she wished me to keep away, why hadn't she locked the door of communication between the sitting-room and the *sala?* That would have been a definite sign that I was to leave them alone. If I didn't leave them alone she meant me to come for a purpose — a purpose now represented by the super-subtle inference that to oblige me she had unlocked the secretary. She hadn't left the key, but the lid would probably move if I touched the button. This possibility pressed me hard and I bent very close to judge. I didn't propose to do anything, not even — not in the least — to let down the lid; I only wanted to test my theory, to see if the cover *would* move. I touched the button with my hand — a mere touch would tell me; and as I did so — it is embarrassing for me to relate it — I looked over my shoulder. It was a chance, an instinct, for I had really heard nothing. I almost let my luminary drop and certainly I stepped back, straightening myself up at what I saw. Juliana stood there in her night-dress, by the doorway of her room, watching me; her hands were raised, she had lifted the everlasting curtain that covered half her face, and for the first, the last, the only time I beheld her extraordinary eyes. They glared at me; they were like the sudden drench, for a caught burglar, of a flood of gaslight; they made me horribly ashamed. I never shall forgot her strange little bent, white, tottering figure, with its lifted head, her attitude, her expression; neither shall I forget the tone in which as I turned, looking at her, she hissed out passionately, furiously:

'Ah, you publishing scoundrel!'

I can't now say what I stammered to excuse myself, to explain; but I went toward her to tell her I meant no harm. She waved me off with her old hands, retreating before me in horror; and the next thing I knew she had fallen back with a quick spasm, as if death had descended on her, into Miss Tina's arms.

9

I left Venice the next morning, directly on learning that my hostess had not succumbed, as I feared at the moment, to the shock I had given her — the shock I may also say she had given me. How in the world could I have supposed her capable of getting out of bed by herself? I failed to see Miss Tina before going; I only saw the *donna*, whom I entrusted with a note for her younger mistress. In this note I mentioned that I should be absent but a few days. I went to Treviso, to Bassano, to Castelfranco; took walks and drives and looked at musty old churches with ill-lighted pictures; I spent hours seated smoking at the doors of cafés, where there were flies and yellow curtains, on the shady side of sleepy little squares. In spite of these pastimes, which were mechanical and perfunctory, I scantily enjoyed my travels: I had had to gulp down a bitter draught and couldn't get rid of the taste. It had been devilish awkward, as the young men say, to be found by Juliana in the dead of night examining the attachment of her bureau; and it had not been less so to have to believe for a good many hours after that it was highly probable I had killed her. My humiliation galled me, but I had to make the best of it, had, in writing to Miss Tina, to minimise it, as well as account for the posture in which I had been discovered. As she gave me no word of answer I couldn't know what impression I made on her. It rankled for me that I had been called a publishing scoundrel, since certainly I did publish and no less certainly hadn't been very delicate. There was a moment when I stood convinced that the only way to purge my dishonour was to take myself straight away on the instant; to sacrifice my hopes and relieve the two poor women for ever of the oppression of my intercourse. Then I reflected that I had better try a short absence first, for I must already have had a sense (unexpressed and dim) that in disappearing completely it wouldn't be merely my own hopes I should condemn to extinction. It would perhaps answer if I kept dark long enough to give the elder lady time to believe herself rid of me. That she would wish to be rid of me after this — if I wasn't rid of her — was now not to be doubted; that midnight monstrosity would have cured her of the disposition to put up with my company for the sake of my dollars. I said to myself that after all I couldn't abandon Miss Tina and I continued to say this even while I noted that she quite ignored my earnest request — I had given her two or three addresses, at little towns, *poste restante* — for some sign of her actual state. I would have made my servant write me news but that he was unable to manage a pen. Couldn't I measure the scorn of Miss Tina's silence — little disdainful as she had ever been? Really the soreness pressed; yet if I had scruples about going back I had others about not doing so, and I wanted to put myself on a better footing. The end of it was that I did return to Venice on the twelfth day; and as my gondola gently bumped against the place steps a fine palpitation of suspense showed me the violence my absence had done me.

I had faced about so abruptly that I hadn't even telegraphed to my servant. He was therefore not at the station to meet me, but he poked out his head from an upper window when I reached the house. 'They have put her into earth, *quella vecchia*,' he said to me in the lower hall while he shouldered my valise; and he grinned and almost winked as if he knew I should be pleased with his news.

'She's dead!' I cried, giving a very different look.

'So it appears, since they've buried her.'

'It's all over then? When was the funeral?'

'The other yesterday. But a funeral you

could scarcely call it, signore: *roba da niente* — *un piccolo passeggio brutto* of two gondolas. *Poveretta!*' the man continued, referring apparently to Miss Tina. His conception of funerals was that they were mainly to amuse the living.

I wanted to know about Miss Tina, how she might be and generally where; but I asked him no more questions till we had got upstairs. Now that the fact had met me I took a bad view of it, especially of the idea that poor Miss Tina had had to manage by herself after the end. What did she know about such arrangements, about the steps to take in such a case? *Poveretta* indeed! I could only hope the doctor had given her support and that she hadn't been neglected by the old friends of whom she had told me, the little band of the faithful whose fidelity consisted in coming to the house once a year. I elicited from my servant that two old ladies and an old gentleman had in fact rallied round Miss Tina and had supported her — they had come for her in a gondola of their own — during the journey to the cemetery, the little red-walled island of tombs which lies to the north of the town and on the way to Murano. It appeared from these signs that the Misses Bordereau were Catholics, a discovery I had never made, as the old woman couldn't go to church and her niece, so far as I perceived, either didn't or went only to early mass in the parish before I was stirring. Certainly even the priests respected their seclusion; I had never caught the whisk of the *curato's* skirt. That evening, an hour later, I sent my servant down with five words on a card to ask if Miss Tina would see me for a few moments. She was not in the house, where he had sought her he told me when he came back, but in the garden walking about to refresh herself and picking the flowers quite as if they belonged to her. He had found her there and she would be happy to see me.

I went down and passed half an hour with poor Miss Tina. She had always had a look of musty mourning, as if she were wearing out old robes of sorrow that wouldn't come to an end; and in this particular she made no different show. But she clearly had been crying, crying a great deal — simply satisfyingly, refreshingly, with a primitive, retarded sense of solitude and violence. But she had none of the airs or graces of grief, and I was almost surprised to see her stand there in the first dusk with her hands full of admirable roses and smile at me with reddened eyes. Her white face, in the frame of her mantilla, looked longer, leaner than usual. I hadn't doubted her being irreconcilably disgusted with me, her construing I ought to have been on the spot to advise her, to help her; and, though I believed there was no rancour in her composition and no great conviction of the importance of her affairs, I had prepared myself for a change in her manner, for some air of injury and estrangement, which should say to my conscience: 'Well, you're a nice person to have professed things!' But historic truth compels me to declare that this poor lady's dull face ceased to be dull, almost ceased to be plain, as she turned it gladly to her late aunt's lodger. That touched him extremely and he thought it simplified his situation until he found it didn't. I was as kind to her that evening as I knew how to be, and I walked about the garden with her as long as seemed good. There was no explanation of any sort between us; I didn't ask her why she hadn't answered my letter. Still less did I repeat what I had said to her in that communication; if she chose to let me suppose she had forgotten the position in which Miss Bordereau had surprised me and the effect of the discovery on the old woman, I was quite willing to take it that way: I was grateful to her for not treating me as if I had killed her aunt.

We strolled and strolled, though really not much passed between us save the recognition of her bereavement, conveyed in my manner and in the expression she had of depending on me now, since I let her see I still took an interest in her. Miss Tina's was no breast for the pride or the pretence of independence; she didn't in the least suggest that she knew at present what would become of her. I forbore to press on that question, however, for I certainly was not prepared to say that I would take charge of her. I was cautious; not ignobly, I think, for I felt her knowledge of life to be so small that in her unsophisticated vision there would be no reason why — since I seemed to pity her — I shouldn't somehow look after her. She told me how her aunt had died, very peacefully at the last, and how everything had been done afterwards by the care of her good friends — fortunately, thanks to me, she said, smiling, there was money in the house. She repeated that when once the 'nice' Italians like you they are your friends for life, and when we had gone into this she asked me about my *giro*, my impressions, my adventures, the places I had seen. I told her what I could, making it up partly, I'm afraid, as in my disconcerted state I had taken little in; and after she had heard me she exclaimed, quite as if she had forgotten her aunt and her sorrow 'Dear, dear, how much I should like to do such things — to take an amusing little journey!' It came over me for the moment that I ought to propose some enterprise, say I would accompany her anywhere she liked; and I remarked at any rate that a pleasant excursion — to give her a change — might be managed: we would think of it, talk it over. I spoke never a word of the Aspern documents, asked no questions as to what she had ascertained or what had otherwise happened with regard to them before Juliana's death. It wasn't that I wasn't on pins and needles to know, but that I thought it more decent not to show greed again so soon after the catastrophe. I hoped she herself would say something, but she never glanced that way, and I thought this natural at the time. Later on, however, that night, it occurred to me that her silence was matter for suspicion; since if she had talked of my movements, of anything so detached as the Giorgione at Castelfranco, she might have alluded to what she could easily remember was in my mind. It was not to be supposed that the emotion produced by her aunt's death had blotted out the recollection that I was interested in that lady's relics, and I fidgeted afterwards as it came to me that her reticence might very possibly just mean that no relics survived. We separated in the garden — it was she who said she must go in; now that she was alone on the *piano nobile* I felt that (judged at any rate by Venetian ideas) I was on rather a different footing in regard to the invasion of it. As I shook hands with her for good-night I asked her if she had some general plan, had thought over what she had best do. 'Oh yes, oh yes, but I haven't settled anything yet,' she replied quite cheerfully. Was her cheerfulness explained by the impression that I would settle for her?

I was glad the next morning that we had neglected practical questions, as this gave me a pretext for seeing her again immediately. There was a practical enough question now to be touched on. I owed it to her to let her know formally that of course I didn't expect her to keep me on as a lodger, as also to show some interest in her own tenure, what she might have on her hands in the way of a lease. But I was not destined, as befell, to converse with her for more than an instant on either of these points. I sent her no message; I simply went down to the *sala* and walked to and fro there. I knew she would come out; she would promptly see me accessible. Somehow I preferred not to be shut up with her; gardens and big halls seemed better places to talk. It was a splendid morning, with something in the air that told of the waning of the long Venetian summer; a freshness from the sea that stirred the flowers in the garden and made a pleasant draught in the house, less shuttered and darkened now than when the old woman was alive. It was the beginning of autumn, of the end of the golden months. With this it was the end of my experiment — or would be in the course of half an hour, when I should really have learned that my dream had been reduced to ashes. After that there would be nothing left for me but to go to the station; for seriously — and as it struck me in the morning light — I couldn't linger there to act as guardian to a piece of middle-aged female helplessness. If she hadn't saved the papers wherein should I be indebted to her? I think I winced a little as I asked myself how much, if she *had* saved them, I should have to recognise and, as it were, reward such a courtesy. Mightn't that service after all saddle me with a guardian-ship? If this idea didn't make me more uncomfortable as I walked up and down it was because I was convinced I had nothing to look to. If the old woman hadn't destroyed everything before she pounced on me in the parlour she had done so the next day.

It took Miss Tina rather longer than I had expected to act on my calculation; but when at last she came out she looked at me without surprise. I mentioned I had been waiting for her and she asked why I hadn't let her know. I was glad a few hours later on that I had checked myself before remarking that a friendly intuition might have told her; it turned to comfort for me that I hadn't played even to that mild extent on her sensibility. What I did say was virtually the truth — that I was too nervous, since I expected her now to settle my fate.

'Your fate?' said Miss Tina, giving me a queer look; and as she spoke I noticed a rare change in her. Yes, she was other than she had been the evening before — less natural and less easy. She had been crying the day before and was not crying now, yet she struck me as less confident. It was as if something had happened to her during the night, or at least as if she had thought of something that troubled her — something in particular that affected her relations with me, made them more embarrassing and more complicated. Had she simply begun to feel that her aunt's not being there now altered my position?

'I mean about our papers. Are there any? You must know now.'

'Yes, there are a great many; more than I supposed.' I was struck with the way her voice trembled as she told me this.

'Do you mean you've got them in there — and that I may see them?'

'I don't think you can see them,' said Miss Tina, with an extraordinary expression of entreaty in her eyes, as if the dearest hope she had in the world now was that I wouldn't take them from her. But how could she expect me to make such a sacrifice as that after all that had passed between us? What had I come back to Venice for but to see them, to take them? My joy at learning they were still in existence was such that if the poor woman had gone down on her knees to beseech me never to mention them again I would have treated the proceeding as a bad joke. 'I've got them but I can't show them,' she lamentably added.

'Not even to me? Ah, Miss Tina!' I broke into a tone of infinite remonstrance and reproach.

She coloured and the tears came back to her eyes; I measured the anguish it cost her to take such a stand which a dreadful sense of duty had imposed on her. It made me quite sick to find myself confronted with that particular obstacle; all the more that it seemed to me I had been distinctly encouraged to leave it out of account. I quite held Miss Tina to have assured me that if she had no greater hindrance than that — ! 'You don't mean to say you made her a death-bed promise? It was precisely against your doing anything of that sort that I thought I was safe. Oh, I would rather she had burnt the papers outright than have to reckon with such a treachery as that.'

'No, it isn't a promise,' said Miss Tina.

'Pray what is it, then?'

She hung fire, but finally said: 'She tried to burn them, but I prevented it. She had hid them in her bed.'

'In her bed — ?'

'Between the mattresses. That's where she put them when she took them out of the trunk. I can't understand how she did it, because Olimpia didn't help her. She tells me so, and I believe her. My aunt only told her afterwards, so that she shouldn't undo the bed — anything but the sheets. So it was very badly made,' added Miss Tina simply.

'I should think so! And how did she try to burn them?'

'She didn't try much; she was too weak those last days. But she told me — she charged me. Oh, it was terrible! She couldn't speak after that night. She could only make signs.'

'And what did you do?'

'I took them away. I locked them up.'

'In the secretary?'

'Yes, in the secretary,' said Miss Tina, reddening again.

'Did you tell her you'd burn them?'

'No, I didn't — on purpose.'

'On purpose to gratify me?'

'Yes, only for that.'

'And what good will you have done me if after all you won't show them?'

'Oh, none. I know that — I know that,' she dismally sounded.

'And did she believe you had destroyed them?'

'I don't know what she believed at the last. I couldn't tell — she was too far gone.'

'Then if there was no promise and no assurance I can't see what ties you.'

'Oh, she hated it so — she hated it so! She was so jealous. But here's the portrait — you may have that,' the poor woman announced, taking the little picture, wrapped up in the same manner in which her aunt had wrapped it, out of her pocket.

'I may have it — do you mean you give it to me?'

I gasped as it passed into my hand.

'Oh, yes.'

'But it's worth money — a large sum.'

'Well!' said Miss Tina, still with her strange look.

I didn't know what to make of it, for it could scarcely mean that she wanted to bargain like her aunt. She spoke as for making me a present.

'I can't take it from you as a gift,' I said, 'and yet I can't afford to pay you for it according to the idea Miss Bordereau had of its value. She rated it at a thousand pounds.'

'Couldn't we sell it?' my friend threw off.

'God forbid! I prefer the picture to the money.'

'Well, then, keep it.'

'You're very generous.'

'So are you.'

'I don't know why you should think so,' I returned; and this was true enough, for the good creature appeared to have in her mind some rich reference that I didn't in the least seize.

'Well, you've made a great difference for me,' she said.

I looked at Jeffrey Aspern's face in the little picture, partly in order not to look at that of my companion, which had begun to trouble me, even to frighten me a little — it had taken so very odd, so strained and unnatural a cast. I made no answer to this last declaration; I but privately consulted Jeffrey Aspern's delightful eyes with my own — they were so young and brilliant and yet so wise and so deep; I asked him what on earth was the matter with Miss Tina. He seemed to smile at me with mild mockery; he might have been amused at my case. I had got into a pickle for him — as if he needed it! He was unsatisfactory for the only moment since I had known him. Nevertheless, now that I held the little picture in my hand I felt it would be a precious possession. 'Is this a bribe to make me give up the papers?' I presently and all perversely asked. 'Much as I value this, you know, if I were to be obliged to choose the papers are what I should prefer. Ah, but ever so much!'

'How can you choose — how can you choose?' Miss Tina returned slowly and woefully.

'I see! Of course there's nothing to be said if you regard the interdiction that rests on you as quite insurmountable. In this case it must seem to you that to part with them would be an impiety of the worst kind, a simple sacrilege!'

She shook her head, only lost in the queerness of her case. 'You'd understand if you had known her. I'm afraid,' she quavered suddenly — 'I'm afraid! She was terrible when she was angry.'

'Yes, I saw something of that, that night. She was terrible. Then I saw her eyes. Lord, they were fine!'

'I see them — they stare at me in the dark!' said Miss Tina.

'You've grown nervous with all you've been through.'

'Oh, yes, very — very!'

'You mustn't mind; that will pass away,' I said kindly. Then I added resignedly, for it really seemed to me that I must accept the situation: 'Well, so it is, and it can't be helped. I must renounce.' My friend, at this, with her eyes on me, gave a low soft moan, and I went on: 'I only wish to goodness she had destroyed them; then there would be nothing more to say. And I can't understand why, with her ideas, she didn't.'

'Oh, she lived on them!' said Miss Tina.

'You can imagine whether that makes me want less to see them,' I returned not quite so desperately. 'But don't let me stand here as if I had it in my soul to tempt you to anything base. Naturally, you understand, I give up my rooms. I leave Venice immediately.' And I took up my hat, which I had placed on a chair. We were still rather awkwardly on our feet in the middle of the *sala*. She had left the door of the apartments open behind her, but had not led me that way.

A strange spasm came into her face as she saw me take my hat. 'Immediately — do you mean today?' The tone of the words was tragic — they were a cry of desolation.

'Oh, no; not so long as I can be of the least service to you.'

'Well, just a day or two more — just two or

three days,' she panted. Then, controlling herself, she added in another manner: 'She wanted to say something to me — the last day — something very particular. But she couldn't.'

'Something very particular?'

'Something more about the papers.'

'And did you guess — have you any idea?'

'No, I've tried to think — but I don't know. I've thought all kinds of things.'

'As for instance?'

'Well, that if you were a relation it would be different.'

I wondered. 'If I were a relation — ?'

'If you weren't a stranger. Then it would be the same for you as for me. Anything that's mine would be yours, and you could do what you like. I shouldn't be able to prevent you — and you'd have no responsibility.'

She brought out this droll explanation with a nervous rush and as if speaking words got by heart. They gave me an impression of a subtlety which at first I failed to follow. But after a moment her face helped me to see further, and then the queerest of lights came to me. It was embarrassing, and I bent my head over Jeffrey Aspern's portrait. What an odd expression was in his face! 'Get out of it as you can, my dear fellow!' I put the picture into the pocket of my coat and said to Miss

Tina: 'Yes, I'll sell it for you. I shan't get a thousand pounds by any means, but I shall get something good.'

She looked at me through pitiful tears, but seemed to try to smile as she returned: 'We can divide the money.'

'No, no, it shall be all yours.' Then I went on: 'I think I know what your poor aunt wanted to say. She wanted to give directions that her papers should be buried with her.'

Miss Tina appeared to weigh this suggestion; after which she answered with striking decision: 'Oh, no, she wouldn't have thought that safe!'

'It seems to me nothing could be safer.'

'She had an idea that when people want to publish they're capable — !' And she paused, very red.

'Of violating a tomb? Mercy on us, what must she have thought of me!'

'She wasn't just, she wasn't generous!' my companion cried with sudden passion.

The light that had come into my mind a moment before spread further. 'Ah, don't say that, for we are a dreadful race.' Then I pursued: 'If she left a will that may give you some idea.'

'I've found nothing of the sort — she destroyed it. She was very fond of me,' Miss Tina added with an effect of extreme

160

inconsequence. 'She wanted me to be happy. And if any person should be kind to me — she wanted to speak of that.'

I was almost awestricken by the astuteness with which the good lady found herself inspired, transparent astuteness as it was and stitching, as the phrase is, with white thread. 'Depend upon it, she didn't want to make any provision that would be agreeable to *me*.'

'No, not to you, but quite to me. She knew I should like it if you could carry out your idea. Not because she cared for you, but because she did think of me,' Miss Tina went on with her unexpected, persuasive volubility. 'You could see the things — you could use them.' She stopped, seeing I grasped the sense of her conditional — stopped long enough for me to give some sign that I didn't give. She must have been conscious, however, that though my face showed the greatest embarrassment ever painted on a human countenance it was not set as a stone, it was also full of compassion. It was a comfort to me a long time afterwards to consider that she couldn't have seen in me the smallest symptom of disrespect. 'I don't know what to do; I'm too tormented. I'm too ashamed!' she continued with vehemence. Then, turning away from me and burying her face in her hands, she burst into a flood of tears. If she didn't know what to do it may be imagined whether I knew better. I stood there dumb, watching her while her sobs resounded in the great empty hall. In a moment she was up at me again with her streaming eyes. 'I'd give you everything, and she'd understand, where she is — she'd forgive me!'

'Ah, Miss Tina — ah, Miss Tina,' I stammered for all reply. I didn't know what to do, as I say, but at a venture I made a wild, vague movement in consequence of which I found myself at the door. I remember standing there and saying: 'It wouldn't do, it wouldn't do!' — saying it pensively, awkwardly, grotesquely, while I looked away to the opposite end of the *sala* as at something very interesting. The next thing I remember is that I was downstairs and out of the house. My gondola was there and my gondolier, reclining on the cushions, sprang up as soon as he saw me. I jumped in, and to his usual *'Dove commanda?'* replied, in a tone that made him stare: 'Anywhere, anywhere; out into the lagoon!'

He rowed me away and I sat there prostrate, groaning softly to myself, my hat pulled over my brow. What in the name of the preposterous did she mean if she didn't mean to offer me her hand? That was the price — that was the price! And did she think I wanted it, poor deluded, infatuated, extravagant lady? My gondolier, behind me, must have seen my ears red as I wondered, motionless there under the fluttering *tenda* with my hidden face, noticing nothing as we passed — wondered whether her delusion, her infatuation had been my own reckless work. Did she think I had made love to her even to get the papers? I hadn't, I hadn't; I repeated that over to myself for an hour, for two hours, till I was wearied if not convinced. I don't know where, on the lagoon, my gondolier took me; we floated aimlessly and with slow, rare strokes. At last I became conscious that we were near the Lido, far up, on the right hand, as you turn your back to Venice, and I made him put me ashore. I wanted to walk, to move, to shed some of my bewilderment. I crossed the narrow strip and got to the sea-beach — I took my way toward Malamocco. But presently I flung myself down again on the warm sand, in the breeze, on the coarse, dry grass. It took it out of me to think I had been so much at fault, that I had unwittingly but none the less deplorably trifled. But I hadn't given her cause — distinctly I hadn't. I had said to Mrs Prest that I would make love to her; but it had been a joke without consequences and I had never said it to my victim. I had been as kind as possible because I really liked her; but since when had that become a crime where a woman of such an age and such an appearance was concerned? I am far from remembering clearly the succession of events and feelings during this long day of confusion, which I spent entirely in wandering about, without going home, until late at night; it only comes back to me that there were moments when I pacified my conscience and others when I lashed it into pain. I didn't laugh all day — that I do recollect; the case, however it might have struck others, seemed to me so little amusing. I should have been better employed perhaps in taking the comic side of it. At any rate, whether I had given cause or not, there was no doubt whatever that I couldn't pay the price. I couldn't accept the proposal. I couldn't, for a bundle of tattered papers, marry a ridiculous, pathetic, provincial old woman. It was a proof of how little she supposed the idea would come to me that she should have decided to suggest it herself in that practical, argumentative, heroic way — with the timidity however, so much more striking than the boldness, that her reasons appeared to come first and her feelings afterward.

As the day went on I grew to wish I had never heard of Aspern's relics, and I cursed the extravagant curiosity that had put John Cumnor on the scent of them. We had more than enough material without them, and my predicament was the just punishment of that most fatal of human follies, our not having known when to stop. It was very well to say it was no predicament, that the way out was simple, that I had only to leave Venice by the first train in the morning, after addressing Miss Tina a note which should be placed in her hand as soon as I got clear of the house; for it was strong proof of my quandary that when I tried to make up the note to my taste in advance — I would put it on paper as soon as I got home, before going to bed — I couldn't think of anything but 'How can I thank you for the rare confidence you've placed in me?' That would never do; it sounded exactly as if an acceptance were to follow. Of course I might get off without writing at all, but that would be brutal, and my idea was still to exclude brutal solutions. As my confusion cooled I lost myself in wonder at the importance I had attached to Juliana's crumpled scraps; the thought of them became odious to me and I was as vexed with the old witch for the superstition that had prevented her from destroying them as I was with myself for having already spent more money than I could afford in attempting to control their fate. I forgot what I did, where I went after leaving the Lido, and at what hour or with what recovery of composure I made my way back to my boat. I only know that in the afternoon, when the air was aglow with the sunset, I was standing before the church of Saints John and Paul and looking up at the small square-jawed face of Bartolommeo Colleoni, the terrible *condottiere* who sits so sturdily astride of his huge bronze horse on the high pedestal on which Venetian gratitude maintains him. The statue is incomparable, the finest of all mounted figures, unless that of Marcus Aurelius, who rides benignant before the Roman Capitol, be finer; but was not thinking of that; I only found myself staring at the triumphant captain as if he had an oracle on his lips. The western light shines into all his grimness at that hour and makes it wonderfully personal. But he continued to look far over my head, at the red immersion of another day — he had seen so many go down into the lagoon through the centuries — and if he were thinking of battles and stratagems they were of a different quality from any I had to tell him of. He couldn't direct me what to do, gaze up at him as I might. Was it before this or after that I wandered about for an hour in the small canals, to the continued stupefaction of my gondolier, who had never seen me so restless and yet so void of a purpose and could extract from me no order but 'Go anywhere — everywhere — all over the place'? He reminded me that I had not lunched and expressed, therefore, respectfully the hope that I would dine earlier. He had had long periods of leisure during the day, when I had left the boat and rambled, so that I was not obliged to consider him, and I told him that till the morrow, for reasons, I should touch no meat. It was an effect of poor Miss Tina's proposal, not altogether auspicious, that I had quite lost my appetite. I don't know why it happened that on this occasion I was more than ever struck with that queer air of sociability, of cousinship and family life, which makes up half the expression of Venice. Without streets and vehicles, the uproar of wheels, the brutality of horses, and with its little winding ways where people crowd together, where voices sound as in the corridors of a house, where the human step circulates as if it skirted the angles of furniture and shoes never wear out, the place has the character of an immense collective apartment, in which Piazza San Marco is the most ornamented corner and palaces and churches, for the rest, play the part of great divans of repose, tables of entertainment, expanses of decoration. And somehow the splendid common domicile, familiar, domestic and resonant, also resembles a theatre with its actors clicking over bridges and, in straggling processions, tripping along fondamentas. As you sit in your gondola the footways that in certain parts edge the canals assume to the eye the importance of a stage, meeting it at the same angle, and the Venetian figures, moving to and fro against the battered scenery of their little houses of comedy, strike you as members of an endless dramatic troupe.

I went to bed that night very tired and without being able to compose an address to Miss Tina. Was this failure the reason why I became conscious the next morning as soon as I awoke of a determination to see the poor lady again the first moment she could receive me? That had something to do with it, but what had still more was the fact that during my sleep the oddest revulsion had taken place in my spirit. I found myself aware of this almost as soon as I opened my eyes: it made me jump out of my bed with the movement of a man who remembers that he had left the house-door ajar or a candle burning under a shelf. Was I still in time to save my goods? That question was in my heart; for what had now come to pass was that in the unconscious cerebration of sleep I had swung back to a passionate appreciation of Juliana's treasure. The pieces composing it were now more precious than ever and a positive ferocity had come into my need to acquire them. The condition Miss Tina had attached to that act no longer appeared an obstacle worth thinking of, and for an hour this morning my repentant imagination brushed it aside. It was absurd I should be able to invent nothing; absurd to renounce so easily and turn away helpless from the idea that the only way to become possessed was to unite myself to her for life. I mightn't untie myself, yet I might still have what she had. I must add by the time I sent down to ask if she would see me I had invented no alternative, though in fact I drew out my dressing in the interest of my wit. This failure was humiliating, yet what could the alternative be? Miss Tina sent back word I might come; and as I descended the stairs and crossed the *sala* to her door — this time she received me in her aunt's forlorn parlour — I hoped she wouldn't think my announcement was to be 'favourable.' She certainly would have understood my recoil of the day before.

As soon as I came into the room I saw that she had done so, but I also saw something which had not been in my forecast. Poor Miss Tina's sense of failure had produced a rare alteration in her, but I had been too full of stratagems and spoils to think of that. Now I took it in; I can scarcely tell how it startled me. She stood in the middle of the room with a face of mildness bent upon me, and her look of forgiveness, of absolution, made her angelic. It beautified her; she was younger; she was not a ridiculous old woman. This trick of her expression, this magic of her spirit, transfigured her, and while I still noted it I heard a whisper somewhere in the depths of my conscience: 'Why not, after all — why not?' It seemed to me I could pay the price. Still more distinctly, however, than the whisper I heard Miss Tina's own voice. I was so struck with the different effect she made on me that at first I wasn't clearly aware of what she was saying; then I recognised she had bade me goodbye — she said something about hoping I should be very happy.

'Goodbye — goodbye?' I repeated with an inflection interrogative and probably foolish.

I saw she didn't feel the interrogation, she only heard the words; she had strung herself up to accepting our separation and they fell upon her ear as a proof. 'Are you going today?' she asked. 'But it doesn't matter, for whenever you go I shall not see you again. I don't want to.' And she smiled strangely, with an infinite gentleness. She had never doubted my having left her the day before in horror. How *could* she, since I hadn't come back before night to contradict, even as a simple form, even as an act of common humanity, such an idea? And now she had the force of soul — Miss Tina with a force of soul was a new conception — to smile at me in her abjection.

'What shall you do — where shall you go?' I asked.

'Oh, I don't know. I've done the great thing. I've destroyed the papers.'

'Destroyed them?' I waited.

'Yes; what was I to keep them for? I burnt them last night, one by one in the kitchen.'

'One by one?' I coldly echoed it.

'It took a long time — there were so many.' The room seemed to go round me as she said this, and a real darkness for a moment descended on my eyes. When it passed, Miss Tina was there still, but the transfiguration was over and she had changed back to a plain, dingy, elderly person. It was in this character she spoke as she said: 'I can't stay with you longer, I can't'; and it was in this character she turned her back upon me, as I had turned mine upon her twenty-four hours before, and moved to the door of her room.

Here she did what I hadn't done when I quitted her — she paused long enough to give me one look. I have never forgotten it and I sometimes still suffer from it, though it was not resentful. No, there was no resentment, nothing hard or vindictive in poor Miss Tina; for when, later, I sent her, as the price of the portrait of Jeffrey Aspern, a larger sum of money than I had hoped to gather for her, writing to her that I had sold the picture, she kept it with thanks; she never sent it back. I wrote her that I had sold the picture, but I admitted to Mrs Prest at the time — I met this other friend in London that autumn — that it hangs above my writing-table. When I look at it I can scarcely bear my loss — I mean of the precious papers.

We do hope that you have enjoyed reading
this large print book.

Did you know that all of our titles
are available for purchase?

We publish a wide range of high quality
large print books including:
Romances, Mysteries, Classics
General Fiction
Non Fiction and Westerns

Special interest titles available in
large print are:
The Little Oxford Dictionary
Music Book
Song Book
Hymn Book
Service Book

Also available from us courtesy of
Oxford University Press:
Young Readers' Dictionary
(large print edition)
Young Readers' Thesaurus
(large print edition)

For further information or a free
brochure, please contact us at:
Ulverscroft Large Print Books Ltd.,
The Green, Bradgate Road, Anstey,
Leicester, LE7 7FU, England.
Tel: (00 44) 0116 236 4325
Fax: (00 44) 0116 234 0205

Other titles published by
The House of Ulverscroft:

THE TURN OF THE SCREW

Henry James

At an isolated stately home in the bleak English countryside, a young governess accepts the job of teaching two beautiful children whose uncle-guardian wants nothing to do with them — and soon she is tormented by visions of ghosts that only she seems able to see: the former governess Miss Jessel and her lover, valet Peter Quint. Even worse, she comes to believe that these ghosts are corrupting the preternaturally angelic souls of little Flora and Miles. The children deny any knowledge of the ghosts, however; and as the tension mounts, the question looms: are the ghosts real, or does the unspoken terror exist only in the governess's mind?

THE CALL OF THE WILD

Jack London

Buck, a St. Bernard-Collie mix, enjoys a comfortable life of domestication in 19th century California, when one day he is suddenly abducted by a man who sells him on in order to pay his gambling debts. Enduring brutal treatment along the way, Buck finds himself fighting for survival as a sled dog in the unforgiving frozen landscape of the Canadian Arctic. Only his indomitable spirit — and an increasing reliance on his primal instincts — enable Buck to face beatings, exhaustion, starvation and loss. Buck's hardships and triumphs come in unexpected turns — but ultimately the power of the call of the wild cannot be denied . . .

WHITE FANG

Jack London

The Yukon, 1800s. A litter of part-dog, part-wolf pups is born in a remote cave; stalked by famine in the harsh environment, White Fang emerges as the only survivor. Quickly learning that the only law of the land is to kill or be killed, the wolf-dog musters the courage and perseverance to endure cruelty and hardship, becoming a savage, morose and solitary fighter. Yet there is one man, a young prospector, who can see beyond White Fang's vicious anger, and decides that it's time to try to win him over . . .

THREE MEN IN A BOAT

Jerome K. Jerome

There are four of them — George, Harris, the writer himself and that dog, Montmorency — all participants in a boating expedition on the Thames. The difficulties and vicissitudes heaped upon these innocents develop to epic proportions as they experience the hazards of the great English waterway. Their problems are in no way diminished by the outrageous behaviour of Montmorency, who lays waste to several riverside communities in the course of their journey. Full of wit and wry humour, this novel with its madcap adventures and side-line streams of consciousness goes far in describing what it means to be English (and what it means to be an English fox terrier!).

THREE MEN ON THE BUMMEL

Jerome K. Jerome

Having survived the hazards of the great English waterway — plus the outrageous behaviour of *that* dog — in their debut novel, *Three Men an a Boat*, we re-join our heroes George, Harris and Jerome on a bicycle tour through the Black Forest. What is a bummel, you may ask? It is a journey, long or short, without an end; the only thing regulating it being the necessity of getting back within a given time to the point from which one started . . . As the trio encounters misadventures involving transport, the weather, and the usually tranquil locals, chaos and mayhem again reign supreme.